# Fairatella

# Dedication

For my sister, Janice, who gave me wings, and for my children, who are the reason I never give up.

# Acknowledgements

*Fairatella* is a fusion of flavours, of all that I've read, seen and heard throughout my life that is magical; it's impossible to make such a list here. I do feel it's essential though, to make a few acknowledgements.

I'm grateful to my friend the wizard, for believing in me and opening my eyes to another world. Also, working with Disney Licensees as an illustrator/graphic designer proved particularly valuable, being influenced and inspired by so many different stories. And to my children, who indulge me, listening to my inner child voice was fun!

However, this fairy-tale is indeed a tale, it's entirely fictional and the views expressed here are my very own.

# CHAPTER ONE

## *A Furry Tail*

How would you feel, if an evil spell had been cast upon you before you were even born? A spell which couldn't be broken to boot, a spell that actually went wrong, as it was most unexpectedly interrupted just before the chant was completed?

Come to Tivarnia, the magical fairyland, and find out what happens to Fairatella, an unfortunate fairy who endured such a spell. But be careful as you turn these pages, as a fairy might just pop out and get you into all kinds of mischief!

So, let's go back to when it all started, at the very beginning, the day Freakadella, the wicked witch of Tivarnia, cast that evil spell on Bellarosea, Fairatella's mother.

Freakadella was the freakiest witch anyone had ever laid eyes on. In fact, even in the dark no one dared to look at her, or speak her name come to that, in fear of her evil eye. There was nothing feminine about Freakadella. She had a huge crooked nose with several hairy warts, and crooked teeth, too; many were missing, and her lips were chapped and cracked. Her long, pointed chin had so much facial hair it almost looked like she had a beard. Undoubtedly, Freakadella's most dominant feature was her dark shadowed eyes, which were even more emphasised by her over-plucked eyebrows. Since she was goggle-eyed, it was very easy for her to put you into a trance, not that anyone dared to stare at her long enough. Her oversized witch's hat hid her slight baldness. The large, black, crow's feather that decorated her hat added a touch of dark eccentricity to it. The few strands of grey hair that she had were so wispy they seemed to have a life of their own. She liked flipping her long black cape and whisking it to one side as gusts of wind caused havoc wherever she set foot. Not even her cape could conceal her huge backside as it bulged out with unseemliness. She wore black leggings, which had holes in them, and gross hairs stuck out. Although she found it difficult to walk in her high-heeled, pointed boots, she still persisted as they made her look taller. She loved the shiny buckles on them too. With a click of her boots she could summon her messengers, which she found amusing. She was foul-mouthed, her deep voice was unnerving, and her evil chuckle could make even the bravest squirm, so everyone kept their distance from her; even her own messengers feared her. If she ever felt lonely she would have a conversation with her obedient broom. The broom was a she and was very talkative but was never allowed to disagree with her.

Freakadella lived down a wishing well, but only the good witch of Tivarnia, Serena, knew that it actually led to her real hideout, an endless underground cavern. There below, she kept her dragoness, Drakess, chained in a bottomless pit, and as Freakadella was so fond of Drakess's baby dragon, Puffin, she stole it and decided to keep it as her pet. Puffin could just about breathe fire but puffed a lot of smoke, which she thought was cute. She also had two pet fruit bats, Batty and Battier, who always argued; they drove her crazy sometimes, but she put up with them because they were excellent night messengers. Three black crows, Scarecrow, Scab and Scar, her most loyal messengers, guarded the entrance to her lair. Their names, if repeated quickly three times, were also the secret password for entering the well. Freakadella thought it had a ring to it and so she used the word, 'Scarecrowscabandscar' often when conjuring up spells too. A wooden sign which said 'WISHING YOU WELL' hung over the well. Many were fooled and fell to their deaths. The victims were Freakadella's favourite snacks!

Cursed be the day that Batty and Battier flew rapidly into the cavern, eager to inform Freakadella of their latest gripping news. They bumped into one another as their wings flapped hastily and squabbled over whom would tell Freakadella first, as they both loved to be treated with bloody snacks.

Simultaneously they blurted out, "Bellarosea and Silver Foxglove are soon to be betrothed, a wedding, a grand wedding is to be organised!"

They were both very surprised when she didn't utter a single word; instead she turned red with rage. Struck with concern, they gave one another a worried look, then a disappointed one, as no treat was given. They flew away speedily before being scorned by her, and screamed as bats do, "Bat bedtime, time to hang out in the furthest away bat cave, batty bye!"

Freakadella was already having a bad day, but now she was distraught with fury and started to jump up and down; a terrible tantrum overcame her. She was already so jealous of Bellarosea's beauty and popularity, but now she had even won the heart of her precious Silver Foxglove, whom she had had a childhood crush on; it was just too much for her to bear. He was sleek and slick, and everyone called him Silver Fox. Devastated, as she only now realised that she must have been secretly in love with him all this time, she wanted revenge, and badly so.

Screeching and cursing, she swore, "So sweet will be my revenge, all of Tivarnia will shudder!" She smiled sinisterly and out of pure spite she started to contrive an evil spell. Just the thought of conjuring up concoctions and wicked spells calmed her a little. Shortly after, she cackled, "Flipping Freakadella, you're a genius! Waa hahahahaha!" So, pleased with herself, she said, "Bellarosea's first born, shall be the ugliest fairy ever to be born in Tivarnia. Poor Bellarosea will become sick with sorrow and self-blame. A dreadful darkness will come upon her and she will slowly wither away like the pathetic little flower of the likes she is. A spell to chant and a potion to mix!"

Puffin set her black cauldron afire, after several attempts, and puffed away at it with delight as she commanded him to. The cauldron bubbled, and the first ingredients were plopped in: tadpole eyes, wild boar hairs, two chicken wings. She chuckled at the thought of a fairy flying like a chicken, bat skins for slippery skin and added a touch of coal to be sure of darkness, and to darken the soul of Bellarosea's firstborn, a squirmy black eel to add wretched ugliness, as well as bad eggs for smelliness, which reeked. All mixed up with a lot of nasty thoughts, into a nastier broth. It needed to be over stewed until it became sticky like glue, as she wanted it to be a potent potion.

But something was missing, she thought... "Aha! I've got it!" she said, on seeing a bitsy peek–a–boo spider waving his paddle like legs seductively at his lady love spider, trying desperately to get her attention whilst she was jumping about. "A little something for creepiness!" said Freakadella, satisfied with her last choice of ingredient. "What a bizarre peek–a–boo courtship these creepy–crawlies have!" she exclaimed as she scrimmaged around with her claw–like fingers, trying to capture the strange spider as it jumped hither and thither. Impatient, she started to chant her spell anyway whilst pursuing them, playing their extraordinary game:

"Bella, Bellarosea, darkness shall fall upon you.
Doom and gloom shall clothe and smother you.
Then I, the black thorn, shall pierce your
feeble heart.
Not blood, but poison ivy, shall flow swift through
your veins.
A bad seed I shall plant within your barren womb,
The fruit you shall bear, can't be compared,
As by far, she will be the ugliest fairy of them all!
Sick with sorrow, you shall beg for your
dose of sweet
d––."

But before she could say the last word, a stroke of fortune occurred. Serena, the good witch of Tivarnia, just happened to overhear Freakadella chanting the spell. The good witch always kept a close watch over her to see what mischief she was up to. Usually she was disguised or transformed into an animal form. On this particular day, she was transformed into a ginger cat and, with no time to lose had to act spontaneously. The last ingredient, the creepy spider, was about to be dropped into the bubbling cauldron, but the ginger cat leapt over the cauldron, snatched it and gobbled it, just in the brink of time! Freakadella said the last word, "death", with an element of surprise.

The cat said, "Ewe," after gulping it and looked totally repulsed, then went "oooooouch!" when its tail got scorched accidently as it dipped into the bubbling cauldron.

Was the spell now broken? Since the spell had already been spoken, Freakadella could no longer undo or correct it, thereby weakening the spell. At first Freakadella was infuriated by the cat's interruption, but on contemplating the matter further, she realised that Bellarosea's firstborn might not be the ugliest fairy in all of Tivarnia, but she knew that it would be deformed in some manner or other and smiled with a sinister satisfaction. Now, aware that she had something to look forward to, she couldn't wait to see the outcome.

That day a special bond was forged between Serena and Fairatella and, rightfully so, she became her guardian fairy and fairy godmother. Later, everyone believed that the cat's scorched tail was just a fluke of luck, as it was the only possible explanation as to why Fairatella was born with a tail, and a ginger one at that. Who would have thought that a tail could be the beginning of such an extraordinary tale!

# The Death of Bellarosea

Later that fairy year, Scarecrow, Scab and Scar eagerly brought Freakadella the news she'd long been waiting for. She was tickled black and absolutely delighted with herself when she learnt that Bellarosea's firstborn had a ginger cat's furry tail, bushy ginger hair, large, glaring cat eyes and unusually small wings for a fairy, which especially amused her. Other than that, though, she looked like any other normal fairy. In fact, the news inspired her to experiment and create more spells so that all newly born fairies, and all living creatures of Tivarnia, would be born disfigured. This idea alone simply thrilled her. She could foresee Tivarnia as a land of misfits. With everyone having a defect, they would all know how it felt to be different. Her ugliness wouldn't matter any more; it might even be fun, even an honour to be called "the ugliest of the ugly!"

So, as it was foretold, a grave darkness came upon Bellarosea after she had given birth. Sick with sorrow and remorse for the misfortune of her new-born child, she became heavy-hearted; that black thorn of grief pierced deeply.

Not blood but poisonous ivy seemed to flow through her veins. She got weaker and weaker, day by day, her colour, light and beauty gradually fading. As if slowly choked by deadly nightshade, she withered like the beautiful rose that she was.

Silver Fox never left her side, and although he was stricken with grief and self-blame too, he took care of her the best he could. He read her favourite stories to her, hoping he could soothe her pain. She herself was a great fairy teller of tales, the most magical tales anyone could ever imagine. Once Bellarosea sensed that death was approaching, she asked her husband to remove the double heart-shaped locket that she wore around her frail neck and made him promise to give it to their daughter when she matured, as a reminder to always have fairy faith. She knew that the time would come when their daughter would want to seek out her past, and the locket would help her, as it had two hearts that intertwined, always close. Her heart would only ever be a shadow away from her precious daughter's. With a feeble voice, her last dying words were for him also to promise that he would love their daughter dearly and to tell her fairy tales. He sighed heavily and promised to abide by her last wishes.

At that dark hour, touched by his deep melancholy, the good witch Serena, who was this time transformed into a nightingale, gave him a spark of inspiration. Fortune smiled that moment and he said, "She shall be known by the name Fairatella."

Bellarosea gave a faint smile of content and perished forever. Thorn birds sung in sorrow and all of Tivarnia dressed in mourning, except for Freakadella–she was too busy being ecstatically happy!

# CHAPTER TWO

## *Sister Bond*

Shortly after the death of Bellarosea, Silver Fox's hair turned completely grey and from then on everyone just called him Silver. Time passed quickly; he loved Fairatella dearly and he doted on her, which helped his broken heart to mend a little. Whether Silver was a good 'teller of tales' or not, he still narrated with love and was probably the reason why Fairatella told tales in such a higgledy-piggledy fashion, or perhaps it was just the cat in her, which made her change her mind constantly. No one really knew. Nevertheless, she believed she knew them all perfectly, and by heart too. Her father, not wanting to offend her, was reluctant to correct her muddling; besides, it made her even more adorable and he found her topsy-turvy tales amusing, in fact most did.

Silver remarried a few years later as he thought Fairatella needed a mother. He knew no one could ever take the place of Bellarosea but he missed companionship, even though no one was ever alone within a fairy community, as everyone helped each other; he still thought it best to remarry. Furthermore, being the High Helper that he was, similar to a statesman, he thought it improper for a fairy of his position and calibre to be single and considered that the public engagements he organised would benefit from having a female touch, since Bellarosea had always advised him well on such matters. He was a respected figure within the community and highly regarded as a disinterested promoter of the Fae public good. The Fae were all those who belonged to the order of fairies.

Fairatella was glad to see her father happy, but she loathed her mean stepmother Alexmeania, as she showed no maternal love whatsoever and made her do all the chores in the home, apart from cooking. She was always nibbling at something or other as she couldn't quite satisfy her hunger pangs, and her cravings were out of control. For this reason, she was unusually fat for a fairy and not that pretty either. She rarely ever smiled and wore a mean expression for most of the day.

Alexmeania despised Fairatella; she was so jealous that Silver loved Fairatella deeply yet her so little. She always found fault with Fairatella, but she could never persuade Silver to take her side, which vexed her even more. Having a child of their own, she hoped, would help her gain his love and leverage over Fairatella, but she never stood a chance there. He was however besotted with his daughter Daisy. He was happy for Fairatella too, as he knew that having a baby sister around would be good for her. Alexmeania felt rejected, so she started to nibble more until it became an addiction; she'd even nibble at her nails and any other inappropriate substances like Silver's tobacco. He always reminded Alexmeania to look presentable for their engagements, till one sad day when he no longer wished to escort her at all, then she regretted not making more of an effort. She hated not being able to take any praise or credit for all his services to the Fae community, as she was after all a megalomaniac.

Thrilled at finally having a baby sister, Fairatella was happier than ever before. She watched over her attentively as she grew older and they loved one another dearly. They were inseparable. The truth was that Daisy received far more affection from her sister than she ever did from her own mother. So, for that reason, she always took Fairatella's side and defended her whenever she could, which further infuriated Alexmeania!

Daisy had a problem pronouncing her Rs and her Ls and she had a habit of thinking out loud. She easily got giddy and was forever saying, "Oops-a-daisy!" She wore an upside-down sunflower for a hat, a daisy chain around her neck that she had made herself, a short, fluffy dandelion tutu dress, which projected horizontally from the waist and hip, and shabby ballet shoes. But what was different about Daisy was that she was born with webbed feet, and that was the reason she never wanted to take off her shoes. Freakadella had put a spell on her, too, out of pure spite and malice. Them both being misfit fairies made their sisterly bond even stronger.

# CHAPTER THREE

## New Age Fairy

Years flew by and nothing out of the ordinary ever really happened to Fairatella, until she became a teenager, and a restless one at that. She was always waiting for something to happen, but it never did. So, she would flit about looking for adventure yet to no avail, until the day adventure found her, right on her very own doorstep well, window to be precise...

Like most teenagers, Fairatella was going through a phase, a New Age fairy phase, and considered herself trendy. She was enchanting but didn't like to think of herself so. Her ginger hair was usually gathered into a ponytail with flower stems, as it was quite bushy, and she couldn't be bothered to straighten it all the time. She did spike her fringe a little to give herself that punk edge, which made her look mischievous, but at the same time it complimented her heart-shaped face. Although she had a whimsical look about her, her beauty was comparable to none. Her big, green cat eyes were her most striking feature; they were so exotic and mystical that one could get lost in them. At first one didn't notice her porcelain skin, her quaint little snub nose or her bewitching smile. Her lips were unusually thin at the sides but grew fuller towards the middle, which often gave the impression that she was pouting; but when she smiled, little dimples appeared unexpectedly which made her look adorable.

Whatever Fairatella wore, she always looked fragile, having such a slender body, but one was not to be fooled by her appearance, as she really was quite strong and agile too. On formal occasions she dressed in a leotard with a tutu, so she could easily hide her bushy tail, but for everyday purposes she liked to be carefree and usually wore matching shorts and a bust decorated with an exotic flower print. Her fingerless lacy gloves matched her lacy wings, which seemed to be embroidered with fine flowers. She couldn't fly as well as most fairies, having smaller wings than them, and they didn't have a tail to feel embarrassed about or to weigh them down whilst in flight. It was understandable why Fairatella had an inferiority complex. Strangely enough, her oversized, green leaf boots gave her confidence and she felt hip wearing them; and they allowed her to walk with a buoyant street style, not to mention that they came in handy when having to give someone the boot! Even though she was embarrassed about her tail, she was aware that it helped her to balance and even perform acrobatic tricks in the most unlikely circumstances.

That particular day she'd been out collecting poppy seeds. She usually got into all kinds of trouble getting them, but she knew it was worth it, as she believed they had magical powers.

For that reason, she kept them safe in her stem drawstring pouch, and wore it over her shoulder all the time. Poppy seeds were her chocolate substitute; they were non-fattening too. She loved eating, well, popping them actually; she'd throw her head backwards, throw a seed in the air and catch it with her mouth as it fell. One pop of a seed helped her sadness go away and filled a hole in her belly too.

Many poppies had been uprooted that day, and she'd even fought off a swarm of bees and was feeling rather fatigued. So, she meditated for a while, hanging upside down like a bat, using her tail for balance, wrapping it around a tree branch, and clasping her hands together as if in prayer. She was almost glad of the light rain shower and took shelter under some heart-shaped Cyclamen leaves.

As she sat resting on one of the leaves, a sadness came upon her. The rain started to pour down, and she suddenly felt all alone, miserable, and disliked herself. Her appearance seemed to be troubling her even more now.

"Damp, damp, depression. Rain, rain, rain... I must seek a new pair of wings, the ones I have are heavy and drag as I walk. My tail weighs me down, too, it prevents me from flying high. But wings of light cannot be found in darkness..."

Fairatella always felt like she didn't fit in with the other fairies of her age and thought that they made fun of her, and sometimes they did bully her. The other fairies flew with such grace, and she thought she was clumsy. She took one glance at her tail, then; it wrapped around her waist as if to comfort her, and she looked over her shoulder at her wings and said, "Hmph, now I know how a chicken feels." Reflecting upon her predicament for a while, she recalled accounts of some fairies not having any wings at all and having to recite a magic spell to fly on a bundle of twigs. "It could be worse, at least I have wings and I don't have to fly around like a witch on a bundle of ragwort stems," she said, and drew up and dropped her shoulders heavily, wanting to shrug off her burden. Still feeling agitated, she gave a cool flip and flutter of her wings to shake off her troubles for good. Even so, she couldn't let it go because her tail was still bugging her, so she contemplated ways to get rid of it, yet none of her ideas seemed feasible. Before long, she took up her thinker's pose for a little while to help her concentrate. Exasperated by not having any good ideas, she started to bang her head with her fist clenched. "Think, think and think!" She popped another poppy seed, hoping it would give her some inspiration. "What if one of my ancestors was a cat and married a fairy, duh, wait, perhaps cats were fairies. I'm going barmy, that would make me Cat Fairy. Oh, that's just great!" Looking glum, she then said, "There is no solution."

Just then a gentle breeze brushed against her face, and she could hear the whisper of the wind through the leaves. Then it murmured into her ear, "The spell must be broken, it's the only way, Chosen One."

She shuddered a little and said in a trembling voice, "Noooooooo way!"

Then, as if struck by lightning, she shouted, "Blooming hell, I'll be damned, that's it!"

She looked puzzled for a while and thought out loud. "But how do I do that? Who would know what I should do? Who is Chosen One? Where would I have to go?" She quickly popped another seed. "But it's forbidden to ever leave Tivarnia..."

Freakadella had forbidden all fairies from leaving Tivarnia, and to make sure that they never did, she had cast a spell so that the borders of Tivarnia were overgrown with enchanted forget-me-nots, flowers which, if anyone dared to cross would be induced into a deadly, deep sleep, by their intoxicating aroma. So, with the passing of time, fairies would soon be forgotten since they could no longer visit children on the other side. She knew how easily Earthlings forgot, but what could she do?

"I don't want to belong to a forgotten species. I must think of something. I need to organise a fairy awareness campaign or other; we need to have the recognition we deserve. Children need to be reminded just how awesome we are. Some don't know we still exist, let alone what a flipping fairy is! United, surely, we can achieve anything, our spirit, our inner glow, our power comes from within, if combined... Yeah, Fairy Power, Fairy Mania! What a cool idea!"

Fairies were pure light and energy, and that was why Earthlings got light-headed and giddy when they were around. They had existed from the beginning of time. No one actually knew where fairies came from and perhaps no one would. Some said they came to be when a star or comet exploded and shattered into a million pieces, or that they were not even from this world but another galaxy. Others believed that the first fairies, the Elders, were fallen angels. But what Fairatella did know for sure was that as long as children believed in fairies, Freakadella's magical powers could still be harnessed. If that dreadful day ever came, when the Fae were to lose their power and Tivarnia were to cease being a wish kingdom, then there would be sheer pandemonium, as Freakadella's dark magic would be so powerful that it would make her invincible.

Little did she know, it was her destiny to prevent that from ever happening.

Her thoughts were disrupted by the sound of heavy thunder and lightning lighting up the sky like she'd never seen before. She sensed that something unexpected was about to happen; she had that gut feeling, the kind she was never wrong about. Suddenly, she remembered that Daisy was terrified of thunderstorms, so she decided to head back home to comfort her. She also didn't want to catch a chill as she hated sneezing and that was why she always stayed away from pepper too. The rain started to pelt down, so she flew as fast as she could and chose a path sheltered by trees so as not to get soaked, but it wasn't long before the rain stopped. Strangely enough, as she looked back over her shoulder down into the valley below, she saw that the thunderstorm still hadn't ceased, and then she realised that it had only rained on the spot where she had been collecting poppy seeds. *That's odd*, she thought, *Something is surely going to happen.* She proceeded swiftly.

On her way home to Milky Brooks, she heard a commotion coming from the distance; some of her so-called friends sounded ecstatic, titivating enthusiastically and making a big fuss over someone, so she flew closer to the lily pond where they were all hanging out to eavesdrop. Trying not to draw attention to herself, she hid behind the old willow tree, whose drooping branches leaned into the pond. On looking closer, she saw that it was Azaar that they were all making a fuss over. Azaar was the heart-throb of Milky Brooks. *He acts like he's every fairy's heart-throb*, she thought. He was a little younger than she was, but he was very tall for his age. His large fine wings caught her eye and she felt envious; she also noticed how dashingly handsome he was, but he had an air of arrogance about him that she didn't like. Still, she thought he was refined and as alluring as smoke! She overheard that he'd just got back from Big Lake, as he'd been staying at his wealthy relatives' mansion place, whilst he attended the coaching school for good manners and etiquette, where all the affluent young fairies went. He had everyone mesmerised with his Big Lake adventures; something told her that he liked being the big fish in a little pond.

Out of the blue, she sneezed: "Achoo! Achoo!" Everyone went silent and all eyes were now on her. She awkwardly stepped out from behind the tree and, not wanting to look conspicuous, said, "Oh, what a flibberty gibbert, I do believe I didn't notice you all there. I was so engrossed in trying to find my, err..." she was making it up as she went along. "Pet, yes, yes, my pet, err... Mr. Mumble Bee!"

"Huh?" They all looked at her with disbelief.

"He's unusually small for a bumblebee you see, err... thumble, I mean thimble size, actually, err... terribly hard to find you know." She hoped that she had sounded convincing.

After hearing their previous conversation, she thought she'd better act prim and proper and said, "Jolly good old chap is Mr. Mumble, if it wasn't for his, err... mumblings, and he also, err... mumbles instead of talking, ha, ha!"

They all answered in harmony. "Oooooh right!"

"Anyway, I forgot my manners. Greetings, fellow fairies," said Fairatella politely.

"Good wishes," they all replied.

Then Azaar said, "You have flowered, Fairatella, since I last saw you, you are fairer than ever."

Suddenly, Fairatella noticed her tail reflection in the pond next to her and desperately tried to hide it by stuffing it in the back of her shorts. As she blushed with embarrassment, she prayed for a hole to open in the ground before her, and swallow her up, or just to disappear into thin air like magic.

Then Azaar said, "What appears to be the trouble, Fairatella?" He was trying not to smile.

One of her so-called friends shouted, "Cat gotcha tongue?"

Fairatella answered, "No, err, jolly decent of you to notice." She screwed up her snub nose in contempt.

Azaar, amused and smitten by her charm, fixed his eyes on her, which made her feel even more nervous.

She responded by saying, "Oh my, look at the time, I must dash, my little sister awaits me." She bade him, and her so-called friends farewell hastily.

Before she had the chance to leave, Azaar called out, "Wait, Fairatella, I'm having a homecoming party tomorrow evening, just a small gathering. I would be delighted if you could come?"

"Ooh, err, I don't, err... I think I'm busy then, err... I mean, I know I'm busy, so many chores to do, you know! Oh, and I've just remembered, I have to take care of my little sister too."

Azaar, even more determined now, said, "I insist that you bring your sister too."

Fairatella, surprised, answered vaguely. "Well, we'll see what tomorrow brings, shall we?" She bade him a fairy goodbye. She dashed off, hoping that her tail wasn't noticeable, and whilst flying sideways she almost bumped into a sycamore tree. She composed herself, shrugged her shoulders, and then flew away as fast as she could. Azaar was intrigued, as he found her delightful and anticipated their next reunion with great enthusiasm. Fairatella, on the other hand, felt humiliated and she cursed herself all the way home.

"Huh, seems like a shallow Hal to me anyway. I would seek a more sensitive fairy, that's if I was looking, which I'm not, but if I were, I would want a meaningful relationship. So there, Azaar of Big Lake... Big Lake my pussy tail!" Her tail stroked her face and she flicked it away and said angrily, "Poppycock, one thing's for sure, this tail has got to go, it's ruining my image!"

# CHAPTER FOUR

## *Milky Brooks*

Milky Brooks was a peaceful and picturesque fairy village beyond compare, as a brook flowed right through it, ornamented with floating almond blossoms that drifted along the surface. From the Milky Brook spring, milk and honey flowed in abundance and provided for all the fairy community living there. Triple Wish Falls was the brook's jewel, and sparkly water cascaded down into Sanctuary Pond. One could cross the pond by the Kissing Stones, also used as a place for courting or by the Rainbow Bridge. At the other side of the bridge were a few stone steps which, if you followed, lead to Fairatella's home, The Tree That Was, the remains of an old hollow, which once was a most beautiful magnolia tree before it became diseased. Some believed it was Freakadella's doing as its beauty offended her. It was considered a sacred place; Serena the good witch had surrounded it with an invisible curtain to keep out the evil eye. At night it looked magical, lit up by tea lights.

      The bedrooms were actually old lanterns that hung from the trees' broken branches, and they swayed when the wind blew. Fairatella's parents occupied the largest bedroom, which was opposite to hers. She shared a dainty room with Daisy, but Fairatella didn't mind at all, as she could keep watch over her. There were three further spare rooms, but since Alexmeania wasn't hospitable, she refused to have guests staying overnight. The rest of the rooms could be found within the tree's hollow; it was a cosy, rustically furnished little house. They had rooms with a view that overlooked the pond; the back view was pleasing too, rural countryside as far as the eye could see. Milky Brooks had boundless scenic routes to discover. From the top of the house you could see beyond the lush green garden to Bluebell Banks, and even Yellow Meadows in the far distance, which seemed to mingle with the sun at midday. Behind the Tree That Was, Fairatella had her own private swimming pool, which was really a puddle, but no one could tell her that, and at the side of their house was a small fishpond. Fairatella's friend the tadpole lived there.

Before going home, Fairatella decided to drop by and see her old friend the tadpole. He too was a victim of Freakadella's black magic; he had strange spots which looked like measles, and he believed that he would never grow into a frog. She couldn't quite remember the tale about the boy who never grew old and couldn't make up her mind what to call him, Peter Pole, or Tad Pan, so she just called him Pan for short. Pan was very happy to see her and swam around in circles with enthusiasm. She sat down beside the pond, took off her boots and made circles with her toes too. She let him tickle her toes, which made her giddy. Whilst watching butterflies flutter by, she roughly related her eventful day to Pan.

Then the most extraordinary thing happened. She heard a buzz in her ear, and just before she was going to flick it away, it spoke: "How zzzzz do you do, I'm Mr. Mmmm Mumble Bee," it said, in a very mumbled voice.

Fairatella's mouth gaped open, and she looked astonished and said, "Fiddlesticks, you're a figment of my imagination, I made you up just a while ago to get myself out of an awkward spot." She rubbed her eyes, hoping it would go away.

Instead it gave her a big cheesy grin and said without taking a breath, "Mr Mumble Bee at your services, Chosen One."

She looked at Pan and then at Mr. Mumble Bee and realised that Pan could see him too. Confused she asked, "What do you mean, Chosen One?"

"Oh, never you mind, all will be told in good time." He answered.

"Huh?" she replied. She noticed he talked nasally and snuffled a lot.

Daisy interrupted her chain of thought by calling out to her and asking where she had been all day. Jumping at the chance to get out of an awkward situation, she said, "Gotta dash," but Mr. Mumble Bee followed her, which she found most irritating. She was starting to believe she was losing her mind. "Oh humbug!" she exclaimed, exasperated.

Daisy threw herself at Fairatella and hugged her tightly around her waist and complained about being left alone all day.

"Alone," replied Fairatella. "But where are our parents?"

Daisy explained to her that they had been busy in the garden all day cutting down rhubarb, as it was obstructing their view, and other odd jobs. Then Daisy let go of her all of a sudden and tried to look cross with her. She straightened her sunflower hat and said, "Oops-a-daisy." She composed herself, then said, "I'm a big girl now, next time Daisy comes too!"

Fairatella smiled, picked her up and went to sit down on the sofa with her. The sofa was once a pincushion and still had holes from where the needles had been stuck. Daisy put her head on her sister's lap and grabbed her hand and placed it on her head, indicating that she wanted to be stroked. Fairatella did so, and with her tail she gingerly stroked Daisy's back with her tail too. Daisy told her she was feeling exhausted, as she'd been in the back garden all day, making new daisy chains. Fairatella mentioned Poppy Valley, the thunderstorm, and Azaar's return, and was just about to tell her about her imaginary Mr. Mumble Bee, who became real, when she realised that he had vanished into thin air without saying a word. *Strange,* she thought. She never mentioned the voice in the wind, as she didn't want to frighten Daisy. She saw that her little sister was in a better mood and she asked her if she wanted to help her think of ways to lose her tail. Daisy was delighted with the idea but tried not to show it, as she knew her sister was sensitive about her tail.

Fairatella jumped off the sofa and coiled her tail around her body like a snake. Daisy giggled. Then Fairatella stuffed her tail in the back of her shorts, made a slight curtsy, then bent over and stuck her behind in the air. Daisy pointed at it and started to get giddy. Then Fairatella sat like a lady on the edge of her thumbnail cup, which was still very large in comparison to her size and used her tail to stir her iced tea. She gave a big sigh and said to Daisy that if she was a man fairy she could cut off her tail but being left with a stump is not very becoming for a girl.

Daisy blurted out, "I've got it, Fweeeze it off with ice!" She had a habit of thinking out aloud. Fairatella responded with a look of dissatisfaction and Daisy said, "Oops-a-daisy, dat would hurt." She looked sheepish.

Then she had another bright idea. "Ooh, ooh or dat dwagon monster... Oops wong again..." She paused momentarily and declared, "I know, wie down on wail way wines and dat twain can run over it!"

Fairatella looked annoyed and said, "Any more bright ideas and you'll be grounded, no playing in the meadow for a week."

Daisy replied, "Oops-a-daisy," and pretended she had hiccups.

Fairatella shouted, "Stop saying that!"

Daisy stormed off in a sulk towards her bedroom. She hid behind her cotton spool bedside table.

Shortly after, Fairatella heard her whimpering like a kitten and pretended not to notice at first. Then Daisy started to sob, so she went to their bedroom to apologise for her harshness and told her she'd had a tiresome day. On approaching, she saw that Daisy was staring down at her webbed feet and Daisy said how ugly they were.

After trying to catch her breath from her jerkiness, she wailed, "Dat fweaky Fweakadella soooo mean!"

That moment was a turning point for Fairatella; she pitied Daisy but also became beside herself with anger. She realised that she had to stop that mean witch once and for all, and shouted, "No more misfit trickery!" At that point, she clenched her fists and put on her foxglove boxing gloves and started to prance around and said, "Floats like a butterfly, stings like wise old Mumble Bee."

Daisy smiled a little, and to cheer her up even more she gave her a ride on her Wurlitzer feather bed, which hung from the ceiling. She spun her around until she got giddy.

Daisy laughed heartily and shouted with glee, "Again, again!"

"What we need is a plan," said Fairatella, giving her one last spin.

"A plan?" Daisy answered curiously.

"Yes, a plan for Freakadella's downfall and to make her undo all of her evil spells."

"Oh," replied Daisy, "Howz we gonna do dat? No one dares to even wook at her!"

Fairatella concentrated for a while and said, "When she's sleeping?"

Daisy trembled and said, "But she grunts and snores like a wild angry boar."

Fairatella nodded in agreement and said, "We need help, Daisy."

"We could ask our fairy godmother?" she replied spontaneously.

"Yes, I know, I know," Fairatella interrupted, and waved her finger at her. "It's on the tip of my tongue... wait, oh yes, like that burnt cinders girl!" Most pleased that she actually remembered the name, she then started to think out loud. "Let's say we do have a fairy godmother, where would we find her?"

"I dunno." Daisy shrugged her shoulders and said, "We could ask Father?"

Fairatella shook her head and said, "This is our secret Daisy." She then banged her head with the palm of her hand and said, "Think, think, think." She popped a poppy seed for inspiration and said, "Hmm, perhaps we have to give her permission to act or something, so her wings can be set free, then she'd be able to help us?"

"Wow, good idea, those poppy seeds sure work," said Daisy.

At the top of her voice, Fairatella shouted, "I grant you permission to act!" They both waited for a while but to their great disappointment, nothing out of the ordinary happened, or so they thought...

Little did they know that their fairy godmother did hear their plea, and they would soon be visited by one of her messengers.

It was way past their bedtime and Daisy asked if Fairatella would tell her one of her tales, and she agreed because she knew it helped her to go to sleep. Fairatella helped her climb onto her lily bed and fluffed up her cotton ball pillow and rested it against the heart-shaped bedstead, which once was an Earthling's brooch, and tucked her in. Her pet spider Spiffy climbed onto the bed, too, and snuggled up right next to her. Daisy decided that she wanted to be told the tale about the Garden Genie and Fairatella started to narrate her tale in the same way she started to tell all of her tales: "Long, long ago, in a not so far away land, there lived a genie, a garden genie to be precise. He lived in a watering can; he was so fond of fairy cakes that he ate them day and night, until he became so fat that he could no longer fit through the waterspout if someone rubbed it to grant three wishes. Trapped inside, feeling lonely and powerless, he went into a deep sulk, and completely bored with himself he decided it was time to fast from eating fairy cakes..."

Daisy had already nodded off at the flip of a wing, but Fairatella hadn't even noticed, as she was so engrossed in telling her tale, which consequently she always took so seriously; she also believed that her voice enraptured her audience. Daisy had fallen asleep with her mouth wide open as she usually did, so Fairatella closed it, not wanting her to catch any flies, then gently kissed her on her forehead. She closed the cobweb mosquito net around her bed and blew out the mushroom lamp on her cotton spool bedside table.

Fairatella flopped onto her white feather bed and gently swung around on it for a while, contemplating the events of the day. Her father popped his head around the door to see if they were safe and sound, and she pretended to be fast asleep, and Daisy was snoring.

"I'm blessed, keep watch over them Bellarosea," whispered Silver, and he sighed and then he closed the door behind him very quietly, so as not to disturb them. Fairatella heard him and a tiny tear rolled down her cheek. She wiped it away wearily; she was too tired to think, let alone sad thoughts, for she was already halfway to slumber land.

Just as her eyelids started to get heavy, she heard the sound of strong wings flapping. Startled at first, she saw that it was a huge dragonfly that was peeping through the bedroom window and looking in at her. She sat upright, in awe of her beauty; her jewel-like colouring was enchanting. Strange it might have seemed, but Fairatella had never seen one up close before; even though it was a new experience for her, she still knew a lot about them, being the great teller of tales that she was. Like the fairy-tales that told of Earthlings who followed dragonflies, because they believed it would lead them to fairies.

She marvelled at the dragonfly's gossamer wings that shimmered as she hovered. After noticing that she had an extra pair of wings, Fairatella wondered if that was the reason why dragonflies could hover in one spot for a very long time. What she thought was very peculiar was that she wore what looked like a pilot's hat with flaps over her ears, which were actually petals. She couldn't help but stare into her huge, compound eyes; there was something quite bizarre about them. The most unusual of all was the magical property of iridescence she displayed on her wings and her long, slender body.

Fairies believed that the shifting of colour, the dragonfly's ability to reflect and refract light and colour, was intertwined with many forms of magic, including colour magic and illusion. It was also related to illusion because of its wings that beat so fast; the fairy eye couldn't see it. What's more, it had the power to guide you through the mists of illusion to the trail of transformation and even travel between different dimensions.

The dragonflies were the fairies' steeds. Fairatella imagined going for a ride on her back before realising she should concentrate on the present situation, which was the reason for the dragonfly's visit, so she did just that. After contemplating the matter, a little further, she concluded that above all, the dragonfly symbolised change because of its ability to fly and to be at ease on water, land and in the air, and since it used its power to control its movements gracefully, it also symbolised change in the sense of self-realisation. She wondered what winds of change awaited her.

Thereupon, the dragonfly spoke rather eloquently and said, "Don't be afraid, Chosen One. I'm a messenger of good will, appointed by your fairy godmother, Serena."

Fairatella, amazed, repeated the dragonfly's words and thought out loud, "Godmother... Serena, lovely name, yippee! So, it's true, I do have one. Wait... Chosen One? That's the third time I've heard that today!" She could hardly contain her excitement and wanted to ask so many questions, but the dragonfly interrupted her, saying that she had no time to waste as she had been followed by one of Freakadella's messengers. She bid her to come closer and to listen to her carefully.

She whispered, "Tomorrow at midnight, be ready, for I shall take you to see your fairy godmother Serena, as requested of me. As it is not safe here, I shall take you to a secret place; it is hidden from all those Serena wishes not to see, so do not mention this to anyone, 'Chosen One.'

Fairatella nodded her head in obedience and said, "Please call me Fairatella, but what should I call you?"

"Dragonfly of course," she replied pragmatically.

Fairatella pondered the name Dragonfly for a long moment; she knew of many tales in which the dragonfly had actually morphed from a real dragon and that dragons also had scales like the dragonfly's wings. That theory delighted her, and she wondered if her visitor had once been a real dragon too.

"Dragonfly is not a very becoming name for one so elegant." She looked at her pensively for another moment and said, "I know, I'll call you Eleganza!"

She gave her a polite smile then answered graciously, "You flatter me, Chosen One."

Fairatella felt agitated and replied, "Why, pray, do you keep calling me that, dear Eleganza?" Although she was flustered, she still tried to remember her manners.

"All will be revealed in good time," said Eleganza, and then she vanished into thin air before Fairatella had the chance to bid her goodnight.

# CHAPTER FIVE

## *Chores*

That night she dreamt that she was falling down a dark well. She felt as fragile as a dandelion being blown in the wind, banging into the sides of the well walls, and bruising herself as she fell down the well shaft. Fearful and in pain, she found herself in a strange cavern; she sensed an evil presence but woke up in a sweat and with her heart palpitating before she could see who or what was so menacing.

The next morning, she awoke feeling apprehensive but also excited, which caused her to have butterflies in her stomach. Her thoughts were still lucid about all that had happened the day before and her nightmare. It occurred to her that it might be a premonition and she gulped, tapped her head with her hand and told herself to be brave and get over it.

She woke Daisy with a wake up "morning sunshine" call and said, "Let's go and have breakfast. I'll make you pancakes with fairy icing sugar."

Daisy reluctantly got out of bed; the thought of pancakes made her feel hungry. She shuffled her feet as she walked, her shoulders limp, her eyes half closed, and couldn't understand why Fairatella looked so lively this morning.

Their parents were already up and sat in the kitchen. Alexmeania was nibbling on whatever she could find, and Silver was paying no attention to her, he was deeply absorbed in thought, reading his newspaper, *Fairy Times*. But soon as he saw his daughters, he brightened up and became very talkative which annoyed Alexmeania intensely. Fairatella whipped up some pancakes in a jiffy, and as they all sat around the breakfast table, her stepmother wanted to know where she had disappeared to all day. She was annoyed that Fairatella had not been around to help with the garden and other chores.

Fairatella poured them tea; she didn't want to spill out her future task, so she answered cautiously, "Oh, I was just collecting poppy seeds."

Alexmeania looked doubtful, and she hadn't convinced her yet, so she persisted further intimidating her and Alexmeania said, "Is that all?" She sensed that Fairatella was on edge.

Fairatella replied nervously, "I bumped into some friends on the way home." Alexmeania still looked sceptic so Fairatella quickly said, "Oh and Azaar has returned from Big Lake," hoping to distract her.

"He has?" Alexmeania's ears pricked up.

Fairatella was relieved and let down her guard. "He invited me to his homecoming party in the late afternoon, and he said I could bring Daisy, too."

Alexmeania, thrilled by the idea, insisted that they went, as she was aware that Azaar was the most sought-after fairy in Milky Brooks and came from a prestigious family too. Also, she liked the idea of having some peace and quiet and relished the thought of having Silver all to herself.

Fairatella realised that she'd got herself into a jam and said, "What about my chores?"

Alexmeania bit off the end of a ginger root and said, whilst still munching, "Oh, never mind about those, you can do double chores tomorrow."

Meanwhile Daisy was overcome with excitement; she couldn't quite believe she'd actually been invited to a party. Fairatella hesitantly agreed to take her, but she saw how happy Daisy looked and she didn't want to be the one to disappoint her.

Alexmeania gave Fairatella lots of chores to do that morning, since she would be free all afternoon, which irritated her, but at least time passed quickly. After she had finished them, her stepmother gave her a list of errands to do, still not satisfied, forever demanding. Fairatella knew it was because she got enjoyment out of making her suffer. Fairatella looked cross and snatched the list out of Alexmeania's plebian hand so Alexmeania, to repay her defiance, conveniently remembered that she wanted her to take bunches of rhubarb and gooseberries to the greengrocer for him to sell. She found the largest basket she could find and stacked it till no more could fit in, and then handed it to Fairatella and sneered at her sarcastically. Vexed, Fairatella bit her tongue and departed without uttering a single word.

On her way to the greengrocers she dropped in to see her aunt the Tooth Fairy; as the basket got heavier and heavier, she needed to rest for a while. On her arrival, she found her aunt very busy building an extension on her Lego-like house, tooth by tooth. She greeted her warmly and immediately offered her refreshment, seeing how exerted she looked. Her aunt didn't get many visitors and since she never lost an opportunity for a good moan, she immediately complained that teeth were hard to come by these days, without asking Fairatella how she was or if she had any news. The future looked bleak to her with the new crisis, as fewer and fewer children believed in fairies, and she worried she wouldn't be able to finish her extension before winter without any teeth. Although Fairatella sympathised with her aunt, she couldn't wait to leave. It gave her earache listening to her grumble non-stop. As soon as she had regained her strength, she bade her farewell and tried not to look so happy about leaving.

She set off up the hill towards the greengrocer's. By the time she had got there, she was almost fainting with exhaustion; she and the rhubarb collapsed in the doorway and gooseberries went rolling down the hill. To hide her embarrassment, she pulled herself together as quick as she could, as she thought everyone in the shop was staring at her. For strength, she popped a poppy seed and then another casually, as she wanted to look unruffled by her mishap. Fortunately, the greengrocer was a kind fairy, and he helped her with the rhubarb and offered her water. She gladly accepted. He paid her with silver dust, and she thanked him and said goodbye.

Fairatella felt lighter and went about her other errands much quicker. Her last stop was to buy bread and fairy cakes, and whilst she was waiting to be served, she thought about her evening ahead and thought it wise to go and find some pixie dust to sprinkle on Daisy, to keep her little sister safe whilst she was absent. *Pixie dust's other magical qualities just might come in handy, too, when facing Freakadella,* thought Fairatella, as she was cautiously optimistic.

She flew as fast as she could with her heavy basket to the spot she knew pixie dust could be found. Over Bluebell Banks and down to Mushroom Woods she flew. There, hidden under some magic mushrooms, she found and gathered enough dust to put in her handkerchief. She tied it up with a flower stem and put it safely in her poppy pouch and looked around her warily; she didn't want to get into any pixie trouble, as they could be nasty, especially if you pinched their precious dust. All done, she dashed off home.

On her arrival she found Daisy beside herself with excitement; she couldn't wait to go to Azaar's party and kept asking if it was time to go. Fairatella, however, wasn't the least bit excited about the party, but she couldn't wait till nightfall to meet her fairy godmother.

# CHAPTER SIX

## *Party Magic*

Azaar spotted Fairatella and Daisy instantly on their arrival. He walked gracefully towards them and greeted them accordingly.

*What airs and graces he puts on,* thought Fairatella, as she couldn't help noticing his smart attire. His white ruffled shirt, like a tide's crest, hit his dark blue Bolero jacket and his tight, fitted trousers made his legs look even longer. He had his hair combed back especially for the occasion, and he glowed, glittered to be exact, as if he had been sprinkled with silver sugar. She looked at him, almost spellbound by his glistening, and awoke when he spoke.

"Enchanted," said Azzar, with one arm behind his back and the other reached out to take her hand. He bowed confidently.

As he was about to kiss her hand, she pulled it away awkwardly and pretended she hadn't realised, making a slight curtsy at the same time, almost bumping their heads together, which made him chuckle a little, but she just smiled back coyly. Daisy curtsied too, but rather clumsily, as she'd been told to do and behave as Fairatella did.

Dazzled by Fairatella's whimsical charm, Azaar thought she was most unlike other fairies, and he found her sweet and simply adorable. The fact that she didn't seem to care less about him made him even more eager to gain her favour. He commented on how lovely they both looked, which made Daisy smile from ear to ear.

Fairatella replied, "You flatter us with your compliments, kind sir." She was wearing her emerald green tutu dress, romantic, soft and bell-shaped; it reached to her ankles, so she could easily hide her tail under all that tulle. The bodice was sequined and sparkled. Green so complimented her pale complexion and ginger hair that she had adorned herself with an emerald green hydrangea flower. She had placed it behind her right ear and her long hair tussled down her back. She wore no jewellery other than her mother's double heart-shaped locket, which she never took off. Inside her clip purse she kept some poppy seeds. *Better to be safe than sorry* she thought; she didn't like having to leave her drawstring pouch at home, hidden. Without her boots she didn't feel so confident when she walked, but she knew they were inappropriate for the occasion, so she wore her red ballet shoes with ribbons tied, criss-cross, up to her knees. She felt a little foolish, as she looked so girly, *but sacrifices had to be made* she thought. Azaar, on the other hand, observed that she didn't realise just how beautiful she really was.

Wearing her best daisy frock, Daisy looked cuter than ever. A daisy tiara decorated her blonde hair. She had made it herself; her hair hung loosely to her shoulders. Her ballet shoes looked a little worse for wear since she never took them off, but she didn't care.

All eyes were now upon them; Azaar raised his arm outwards and said, "After you." They walked towards the other guests including her so-called friends. The party was held outdoors in his enchanted garden, and paper lanterns decorated the trees and blew in the soft breeze. It had grown dark, and candle flames danced and lit up the place, and fairy lights twinkled, magic all around. They passed under an arch ornamented with white roses and followed the stone pathway which led to a white pavilion covered in flowers and fairy lights, hung like garlands and sparkling in excitement. The atmosphere was bewitching, and a sweet aroma filled the night air.

*A fairy gathering smelt like a host of intoxicating flowers,* thought Fairatella, as her sense of smell was stronger than others, and it almost made her light-headed and giddy.

The euphoria of the party made her almost forget that she was to meet her fairy godmother later that evening, but her feet soon touched the ground when she saw her so-called friends standing beside the pavilion. Azaar excused himself before he went over to talk to some of his guests. She recognised Blade wearing his all green outfit as usual; he looked like a blade of grass. He appeared to be complaining about something to Azaar. He was known for his sharp temper, but Azaar cracked a joke and they all burst out laughing.

"Tut, tut, isn't he just hilarious, that's enough to make a cat laugh," Fairatella said, with a tinge of irony in her voice, and Daisy giggled. Fairatella felt obliged to mingle with her friends, too, even though she'd rather have hidden in a corner with Daisy somewhere. She felt nervous and reached out to hold Daisy's hand. Preparing herself not to be offended as she approached them, she never felt at ease around them and wished she could disappear or at least fit in with the rest of the crowd.

It was Tulipa she noticed first, as she was unusually tall for a girl fairy; she had a stalk-like body with a big tulip-shaped head.

If it weren't for her large bottom you'd mistake her for a tulip. She had a big mouth, too, and she was very lippy and bossy; all the other fairies acknowledged her as the leader of the pack. Her words could be hurtful and for that reason she wasn't such a good friend as she made out to be.

As soon as she saw Fairatella she said sarcastically, "My oh my, look what the cat dragged in."

Fairatella responded promptly, "Ha, ha, not funny."

Tulipa replied, "Little funny honey?"

"Don't you honeysuckle me," Fairatella said, annoyed.

"Ooh, cat mysterious, cat be weird," huffed Tulipa, enjoying provoking her.

At this point Daisy butted in and said, "Tulipa taller than anyone I know." She looked up at her with her mouth wide open.

Fairatella muttered, "She'd fall harder than anyone I know too, if I tripped her with my tail."

Daisy giggled.

Tulipa pretended she hadn't heard and said, "What tail? Stop telling tales, Cinderella."

Fairatella ground her teeth and almost bit her tongue, then said, "I'm flipping Fairatella and you sure can spin a yarn!"

"Poppycock don't get your wings in a twist honey," Tulipa said, as she saw that she was winding her up.

Daisy could feel the tension; she wanted to stick up for her sister and whispered in Fairatella's ear, "Tell her she's eating too many fairy cakes like the garden genie."

Fairatella gave a smile of satisfaction then backfired at Tulipa, "See, you've been eating too many fairy cakes, your bottom has blossomed like that big head of yours!" She knew she'd hit a soft spot as she glared at her and pierced her lips tightly. Fairatella imagined steam coming out of her ears and muttered to Daisy, "She's so full of hot air, if she let off any steam she'd blow up all of flipping Tivarnia!"

Daisy took one look at Tulipa and said, "Yep, I get the picture." She said out loud spontaneously, "Perhaps a cup of mint tea and a fairy cake?" She then smiled nervously.

Just as Tulipa was about to retaliate, her other so-called friends came to the rescue in fear of the party being disrupted; it was far too early for them to be leaving. They'd been present but had kept silent throughout the quarrel, and now they were desperately thinking of a reason to intervene, but nothing came to mind since they were all dim-witted. It was meddlesome Marigold's bright idea to make polite conversation, and she started admiring all their outfits one by one. "Oh, what a beautiful dress you're wearing, Bluebell!"

Being the busybody Bluebell was, she wanted to know every detail about Marigold's outfit. She stood fanning her face with her ornate feather and looked her up and down. "Oh my, what delicate stitching your bodice has, and surely you didn't embroider it all by your little self?"

Marigold never answered and turned to Jasmine and admired her gown, too, and so forth... until she had bored them all with her petty talk.

Tulipa pretended to yawn. She found her as tedious as a twice-told tale and said flippantly, "What beautiful wings you've got, Marigold... to fly away with!"

Marigold huffed at Tulipa's remark, but she really did have a gorgeous pair of wings, so she didn't pay any attention to her and looked elsewhere.

Fairatella, however, was a little envious of her wings and muttered to Daisy, "Soon they'll be saying what big teeth you've got!"

Daisy giggled and said, "Oh yes, like that Wittle Wed Widing Hood."

Just as Fairatella was starting to feel more at ease, Tulipa suddenly made a nasty remark about her out loud, for everyone to hear. "Where is that tail of yours tonight, Fairatella, hiding under that flimsy tutu I dare say?" she said sardonically.

Fairatella wanted to disappear, as she hated being stared at, and she took a minute or two to compose her thoughts before she replied, "Darn, that was a low blueberry even for her. I didn't know she could be so cruel and callous, now what am I supposed to say?" She tried not to show that she'd hurt her feelings, and then it came to her in a flash. "You're a teller of tall stories, you tell me tattletale?"

At that point Marigold, alarmed, muttered under her breath, "That's my exit cue." She saw that Tulipa was about to retaliate with a vengeance. Wanting to avoid any kind of friction, she turned to her daft friend Daffodila who was always daydreaming and said, "Stop dawdling, Daffodila, let's go and mingle." She grabbed Daffodila by the arm, who was lost in thought at the time, and marched off with her, without her ever realising what had just happened.

Azaar overheard their discussion. He sensed Fairatella's awkwardness and thought that Tulipa was really mean constantly trying to offend her, so he quickly asked for everyone to gather around him as the highlight of the evening was about to commence. He had to improvise as he hadn't really planned for any special kind of party entertainment, but that was a piece of cake for him, for he was known for his sleight of hand; his friends called him the magician.

# CHAPTER SEVEN

## *Party Magic*

All fairies believe in magic. The only difference in the fairy world is that their magic is real; there is no need for deception or trickery of light. They have the ability to do things that normal humans cannot, like teleportation and conjuring up objects, and Azaar could do all of that with ease.

"Can I borrow your glass of dew water for a moment?" said Azaar as he snatched it out of Blade's hand.

"Hey! Now what are you up to?" said Blade, raising one of his eyebrows. He wasn't the least bit amused, as he was still thirsty.

"Magic time, play along with me, Blade," said Azaar, and nudged him.

"Ooh right!" said Blade and hinted that he had understood with a wink. He then shouted as loud as possible, "Fellow fairies, our host and entertainer for this evening, Azaar the magician, the master of illusions!"

Everyone clapped with enthusiasm.

"Tonight's theme..." Azaar paused for a moment and looked like he was deep in thought. After having a marvellous idea, his eyes lit up with a boyish enthusiasm.

"The elements! I'm going to show you all just how magical they really are!"

"WATER! With a few drops of water..." announced Azaar.

First, Azaar quickly uprooted a nearby wilting shrub, and he revived it by sprinkling it with a few drops of water. The shrub wondrously flourished. It grew bigger at remarkable speed, bending the space–time continuum itself. The shrub bloomed with a delicate pale pink flower and then it bore luscious fruit, wild ripe raspberries, one of the fairies' favourite fruits.

He picked one or two and popped one casually in his mouth and said, "Yum, sweet and tangy." Then popped the other. "Delicious!" He then picked a few more and threw them to the nearby spectators, exciting the audience as he did so. "Water, the miracle of life, without it, everything would perish."

Now that he had everyone's attention, he decided to be even more daring. Turning towards the nearby water fountain centrepiece, he raised his arms in the air and concentrated for a moment or two. It was baroque styled, made of marble, and the fountainhead was ornate and shaped like a dragon's head, and water poured out of its mouth quite sensationally. Around the base of the fountain, snapdragon flowers flourished and were forever in bloom due to the cool, magical waters. With his hands outstretched, Azaar summoned the water from the dragon's mouth, drawing it towards him, beckoning it with his long fingers. The pouring water started flowing uphill and rotating as it escalated. "Water always finds a way!" cried Azaar, and then he started bending the water by making strange circular movements with his hands and flicking his fingers until he created a transparent water dragon. Translucent dragon's wings sprayed water as they flapped, and an elongated tail splashed as it surged and waved. As the water dragon opened its mouth ferociously as if to blow fire, the audience ducked, but instead they were showered with cool drops of water, thrilling them to bits! After the water dispersed, the dragon disappeared like magic. The illusion was a phenomenon.

"That should've cooled you all down on this midsummer's eve!" Azaar exclaimed.

*What a show off!* thought Fairatella, but she had to admit to herself that it was a pretty impressive illusion.

"FIRE! With a few sparks..." announced Azaar.

Snapping off a branch and grabbing a few silken threads from a cobweb above him, he hastily made his own violin. He played so intensely, and with a fever, that sparks started to fly from the strings and the violin caught fire. Dropping the burning violin, he caught a few sparks in his hands, and the ground around him then burst into flames.

As he walked through a blazing fire, Daffodila awoke from her daydreaming and shouted, "He's on fire!"

The crowd went into a delirium. He lowered his hands to the side and the flames at his feet ceased, but sparks still flew from his hands. Azaar raised his hands in the air for a moment then lowered them and brought his hands together in front of his chest and called out, "I would like a volunteer to assist me with my next illusion... anyone?" When no one volunteered, he saw it as the perfect opportunity for badgering Tulipa; he wanted to teach her a lesson.

Fairies can make others see things that aren't really there, an illusion, but they can't do it to each other without first giving their consent. "Since you're the tallest Tulipa, I spotted you first, and I bet you're a great performer, come along now," Azaar said, whilst beckoning her to approach with his hands afire. At first Tulipa was reluctant, as she didn't like an audience watching her, especially since she didn't know what kind of mischief Azaar was up to, and she was very wary of illusions.

Azaar started to roll his hands around to make a ball of fire. Once he had everyone's attention, he threw the fireball out into the audience. He looked up at the full moon and said, "Magic moon, make fireflies swoon!"

The fireball immediately dispersed like a firework explosion, and the sparks transformed into a swarm of fireflies. He moved his arms backwards and forwards, and then in the direction he wanted the fireflies to move to create more suspense, mesmerising his guests as his arms swayed to and fro. "Fire is active energy, it may burn with joy or anger and it may offer life-giving light and heat or destruction," he proclaimed. He then gave an up-to-something kind of grin and said, "It is also passionate and can warm up the coldest of hearts!"

Suddenly, a precious tulip appeared out of nowhere, suspended in the air, and the fireflies carried it between them very gracefully, swishing it through the air, and then swooped down with it towards Tulipa. They stopped in front of her and let go of the tulip directly above her so that it would fall right into her hands. The audience cheered with delight; everyone was impressed, including Tulipa. Bringing his forefinger to his lips, Azaar urged them all to be silent, "Shush, sssshhhh!"

Feeling flattered that Azaar had chosen her, Tulipa thought that all her friends would be absolutely envious, as he was after all every girl fairy's heart—throb! She smiled and said, "Thank you kindly." She nodded her head and agreed to be his volunteer as she approached him eagerly.

Now he had her consent, he could perform an illusion on her.

"Come closer, I don't bite," said Azaar, flashing his white teeth. Tulipa's knees went weak; she found him dashingly handsome. She was still holding the precious tulip in her hands when she stepped closer to him.

"Earth! With a few grains of soil..." announced Azaar.

He knelt down and filtered soil through his fingertips, kept hold of a few grains and said, "Mother Earth is the foundation for all living things to rise, live and thrive. She reaps what is sown by the other elements and in turn bestows us with a myriad of abundance." Still crouching, he looked up at Tulipa pensively and then said, "Shall I compare you to a beautiful tulip, tall and slender?" to flatter her. She covered her bottom with her wings and hoped he hadn't noticed how large it was.

Azaar looked at the grains in his hand and said, "Take something ordinary..." He threw the soil at her feet. "And make it eXtraordinary!"

Surprised to see that her feet were starting to take root and that she couldn't move, Tulipa got anXious and wriggled about like a worm. She tried pulling at her feet to uproot them but to no avail, as they were firmly embedded into the ground.

"A spring shower to refresh your delicate leaves, my dear?" asked Azaar.

"Huh? Leaves?" answered Tulipa, completely muddled.

"I will take that as a yes! Abracadabra," hollered Azaar.

All at once, a watering can appeared over her head and showered her with water drops, transforming her into a tulip. Leaves sprung from her side, her body grew even taller like a stem and her feet rooted even deeper, but to her dismay her bottom bulged like a voluptuous bulb. She already felt embarrassed about its size, but now it was even bigger, and everyone noticed it. She blushed a tulip red. Scowling at Azaar whilst still trying to uproot her feet, she silently cursed him. A hunch told her that he had made her bottom grow fatter on purpose to make her look like a fool. Azaar initially had hoped that by embarrassing Tulipa, it would make her realise that it was not nice to make fun of other's weaknesses, as she had, but maybe he had gone too far...

Witnessing Tulipa being ridiculed in that manner at first made Fairatella smile from ear to ear, and Daisy's face ached, as she wanted to laugh hard and was trying desperately to hold it in. The fact that Azaar was sticking up for her by teaching Tulipa a lesson pleasantly surprised her. She had never taken him for the considerate type; she had always regarded him as being what she called a shallow Hal. *He must have been eavesdropping on our conversation and contrived a diversion just for me, but why go to all that trouble?* she asked herself. After a short while, though, she sensed that Tulipa was actually deeply offended and Fairatella felt rotten, as she knew exactly how she felt. Since she didn't have a spiteful bone in her body and never sought revenge, she decided to rescue Tulipa from any further ridicule.

To stop the audience from laughing at her, she jumped in front of Tulipa rather clumsily and interrupted Azaar by saying, "I'd like to try now please."

Tulipa heaved a sigh of relief. Taking Azaar by surprise as she volunteered to be the next performer, his concentration was broken, and the illusion was disrupted, but he admired Fairatella's spirit for doing so.

"Your wish is my command, fair Fairatella," said Azaar, and bowed gracefully before her and then whispered to her, "She got what she deserved."

Fairatella gave him a baffled, shame-on-you look, then turned around to face Tulipa. She had never expected to see lippy Tulipa torn to pieces that way and suspected that she wasn't as tough as she made out to be after all. Fairatella gave her a quick wink and a smile of encouragement, and she smiled back at her thankfully before rushing off. Tulipa might never have had admitted it, but she really was grateful to Fairatella for getting her out of a tight spot.

"What kind of *ignis fatuus* shall I perform for you, my dear?" said Azaar, wanting to sound clever and then gave her a flirtatious smile.

Twirling her hair around her finger and with a blank expression on her face, Fairatella just shrugged her shoulders at him. Half expecting him to transform her into a ginger cat, she gulped at the very thought and prepared herself to be ridiculed too. But instead Azaar had something far more spectacular up his sleeve for Fairatella.

"Air!" With a few fluttering wings..." announced Azaar.

The most beautiful array of butterflies flew out from under his sleeves, leaving a trail of glitter behind them. There were hundreds of them, dazzling her with a rainbow of colour. As their wings brushed hers, she felt a tingly sensation; they covered and caressed her wings and lifted her in the air, and she felt lighter than a feather. The flutter of so many wings made her giddy. A soft breeze gently blew as Azaar raised his arms in the air, and then his hands dropped like the rolling of a stone downhill, twirling her as he did so. His hands stopped rolling suddenly and she remained suspended in the air, and he said, "The air carries a message, listen to the wind," before he summoned a stronger gust of wind, which swirled her swiftly around a few times. "Behold the gift of air, without it our wings are useless," he said, and he had the audience spellbound.

Reaching out his hand, Azaar said, "Shall we dance?"

She accepted gladly. His hands wrapped around hers and she felt safe. They just stood for a moment holding hands and their eyes glistened as their gaze met. The next moment they started to waltz around to bewitching music played by an invisible orchestra. Their feet never touched the ground, making them feel ecstatically happy and carefree, but more than that, Fairatella forgot about how small her wings were. The audience cheered and clapped with enthusiasm as they watched the enchanting dance of the butterflies. He whirled her around by the hands so fast that they looked like a kaleidoscope of forever changing colour.

"You're giving me the butterflies," she exclaimed; all the swizzing around was making her too giddy. "Slow down, I feel so dizzy!" she said breathlessly.

On hearing her plea, Azzar put an end to the illusion rather abruptly and they both tumbled to the floor like two shaken leaves. By chance, Fairatella ended up falling right into his arms. He looked her right in the eye, but she just blew her tussled hair out of her face and, whilst trying to catch her breath, she then said, "Woozy?"

Her head was still spinning, and her eyes rolled around. Azaar tossed back his hair and gave her a capricious smile; he felt like kissing her, but after having second thoughts, he decided it was best just to help her up off the floor instead. They both straightened their ruffled clothes and then he took a bow and she made a slight curtsy and the audience applauded.

Fairatella turned towards Azaar and said politely, "If you don't mind, I must go and keep an eye on Daisy."

He nodded his head in understanding and said, "Please do, and thank you for assisting me." After that, to her surprise, he said, "A round of applause for Fairatella!"

Feeling quite embarrassed, she couldn't leave the scene quick enough and tripped up whilst everyone was clapping. Azaar covered for her and hastily announced the last element. "Spirit! With a few specs of dust..."

The audience watched in anticipation as he casually reached inside his pockets, and as he pulled out his hands, a few specs of fairy dust glittered and fell lightly to his feet. With an air of seriousness, he said, "Finally, the Spirit element, or as our elders called it Ether. It is everywhere and nowhere, and it is the force that unites all things and connects us to the astral world."

A ghostly shadow of himself appeared without warning right behind him and then sprang free to the side as a separate, soul-like entity. It copied his actions and even echoed his words. "I need you all to form a circle and join hands."

A fairy circle was formed, and Azaar and his ghostly apparition stood right in the middle and everyone waited in silence.

"Even though we can't exactly see or place Spirit, as it has no physical presence, we know it is there. It's the bridge between our soul and our bodies. There are times when we can reach beyond and touch something greater than ourselves. That is Spirit." He lowered his head after he spoke, and so did his ghost. Bringing his hands together as if in prayer, he then cried out, "Now raise your joined hands high in the air!"

Suddenly, Azaar and his ghost started twirling around like whirling Dervishes, intertwining, sprinkling them all with fairy dust as they spun in repetitive circles. Azaar's spirit lifted and he continued like so till he contacted the divine mind.

He remained focused and channelled his energy as he whirled around, and the fairy dust started to rise, and then it gathered into a glistening cloud above him and the fairy circle of joined hands. A bright flash of light suddenly exploded from the cloud; an explosion of tiny sparks erupted and fell like a cascade of fireworks. The night sky above loosened and a flickering aurora emerged, a beautiful light display lighting up the dark sky. A whitish glow flickered like a candle flame when exposed to a sudden draught of air, and a crackling noise could be heard in the still of the night.

Whilst gazing up at the aurora phenomena, Fairatella whispered to Daisy, "Heavens above, looks like someone is flipping a light switch."

Daisy stared in awe with her mouth agape and said nothing. Amazing arcs of light rapidly grew brighter above them and twisted into contorted shapes that swept across the sky. All at once, the arcs merged into one brilliant arc, and at one end, after a shimmer of a rare bluish light, a wonderful star fused. They only got a quick glimpse of a blinding light and then *poof*; it took off at lightning speed. The evanescence of the shooting star made it so hard to capture; one moment it was there right above them, and the next *poof*, it was gone. Everyone was high spirited and stood and gazed up in wonder.

The shooting star roused Fairatella from her trance-like state, and for some unknown reason it made her think of Serena and caused her to look around. She noticed a fairy light go out on the pavilion. *Another child has stopped believing in fairies*, she thought sadly, and sighed. The euphoria of the party instantly wore off for her, as she was reminded of her task ahead, but she was still excited about meeting her fairy godmother later that evening. She almost felt like leaving right away, but she stayed for Daisy's sake, as she didn't want to be a party pooper and spoil all the fun she was having.

Still standing in the middle, Azaar raised his arms in the air and signalled for the flower trumpets to be blown, which got everyone's attention immediately, and then he said, "That's all, fairy folks! Shows over. Let the sacred elements guide us, as they guided our elders before us!" After taking a bow, he then announced that it was time for refreshments. "Do try our fairy punch, the punch of all punches, and I also recommend the elderberry and blackberry jelly. Thank you for coming and enjoy the rest of the evening."

The audience dispersed but the party fever continued.

A buffet of blackberries, wild fruits such as raspberries, which Azaar knew all fairies simply adore, honey straight from the honeycomb, the nectar of wild flowers and many more exotic delicacies were served that night. They drank slightly chilled dewdrops and nectar soft drinks, but mostly the fairy punch. It was a delicious aromatic infusion of elderberries, mulberries, rosebuds and a touch of cinnamon spice and goodness knows what else, all mixed up with fairy dust and a touch of tipsy magic.

Azaar told Fairatella that its stimulating properties were enough to keep a cat awake all day and smiled as he handed her a goblet full. "Let's make a toast to our special friendship," he said, as he raised his goblet.

She did the same and gave him an impish smile and said, "To friendship." She took a sip and said, "Mm, delicious!" As she glanced around she saw that everyone else was having fun, the atmosphere was buzzing again, and it heartened her and made her chuckle out loud. "Fairies sure know how to party!"

Melodious music played in the background as everyone feasted, drunk and got merry. The soft ringing of little bells could be heard as ethereal fairies danced the night away; many had worn them sewn to their clothes and they jangled sweetly in time to the music. They pranced about as fleeting butterflies do, so airy and light, and when the music slowed down, they looked like leaves dancing in the wind, swept to and fro. Fairies truly are the most magical winged creatures of them all. The party slowly drifted into a haze, like a magical dream that flickered and sparkled with stardust.

The night seemed endless, until another fairy light went out on the pavilion, which this time everyone noticed, and the party fizzled out. Fairatella gave a wistful glance at Daisy and said, "Time to go." She grabbed her by the hand and then she bid her so-called friends goodnight.

Tulipa shouted, "Hope to see you around, cat fairy!" Fairatella muttered under her breath, "Not if I see you first." She presumed that Tulipa was acting tough as usual, but then she was nicely surprised to see Tulipa wink and grin at her, showing her that there were no hard feelings between them.

Azaar waltzed over to her and offered his hand and said light-heartedly, "One last dance?"

Fairatella replied awkwardly, "Pardon me, but it's time for us to leave, it's way past Daisy's bedtime."

He reached closer as if to kiss her, but Daisy started to pull at Fairatella's dress, looking dainty and tired. Fairatella considered that she was cramping her style at that moment, so she pretended she hadn't noticed Daisy or Azaar trying to kiss her and backed away from him. But this time, he did manage a quick peck on her hand as he bowed, catching her by surprise. She bade him farewell hastily, and in her eagerness to leave, she dropped her purse unknowingly and the poppy seeds fell out and rolled like tiny marbles all over the ground. Azaar sighed as he watched her leave in a hurry with Daisy. Then, to his delight, in the light of the moon, he saw her empty purse twinkle on the ground and he picked it up, then smiled broadly, because he knew that now he had an excuse to call on her the next day.

# CHAPTER EIGHT

## *Phantasmagorical Night Flight*

Daisy had dozed off and Fairatella had to carry her most of the way home; fortunately, they didn't live far from Azaar's residence. Daisy seemed twice her weight and she was sleeping like a log. Fairatella felt a bit tipsy.

*Those rosebuds can sure excite those taste buds and potent that punch, my head's all fuzzy,* she thought. *But it does stimulate the senses to help keep you awake, Azaar was right, I should have been out like a light myself after my exhausting day.*

She'd drunk more than she should have done on purpose and had forbidden Daisy to drink any at all. Rightly so, the elders called it the punch of all punches.

*Soon it will be midnight, I must rush,* she thought, not wanting to be late for her meeting with Eleganza. Fairatella was so excited about what was in store for her; she couldn't wait to meet Serena. She imagined that Daisy was as light as a feather, so that she could carry her effortlessly, and as swift as a bird. *It's mind over matter,* she thought, and was just about to pop a poppy seed when she realised she must have dropped her purse as she was leaving the party. *Oh well, no time to lose,* she thought. She tried not to think about Azaar and the party, but she did and before she knew it she was home. She almost tumbled through the door and Daisy woke with a start and closed her eyes again as if nothing had happened.

Alexmeania and Silver had waited up for them and asked if they'd enjoyed the party upon entering the house. Busybody Alexmeania wanted to know everything that had taken place, but Fairatella said it was late; she would tell them in the morning about the party, as she had to put Daisy to bed. Fairatella pretended to be exhausted, too, by suppressing a yawn, and she was about to bid her parents goodnight, when Alexmeania approached towards her menacingly, to determine whether or not Fairatella really was exhausted. Alexmeania glared enviously at Fairatella, as she held Daisy lovingly in her arms. Then, most unexpectedly, Alexmeania kissed Daisy goodnight, awakening Daisy from her slumber, with her bad breath. Spontaneously, Daisy pushed Alexmeania away in disgust, which shocked Alexmeania immensely. Alarmed, as to how Alexmeania would react next, Fairatella hastily took Daisy to their bedroom, before Alexmeania could retaliate. She tucked Daisy into bed half-conscious and, out of habit, asked Fairatella to tell her a tale. She did, even though Daisy didn't really need to be told one, but Fairatella had to make sure Daisy was fast asleep before she left.

"Long, long ago, in a not so far away land, there lived a horse called Merry, but he was always so sad because he was only a wooden horse, a Merry-go-round horse, well, a Carousel horse to be precise. He lived in a fairyground (fairground) and dreamed of cantering off..."

Daisy, sound asleep, breathed slowly; Fairatella kissed her goodnight and wished her to be safe until she returned, sprinkling her with a little pixie dust.

She quickly changed into her comfortable everyday clothes, found her poppy pouch, put the pixie dust in the pouch's inside pocket and remembered to drink water, too, as the fairy punch had made her thirsty. She had just made it in time; the clock struck midnight and Eleganza appeared at the bedroom window as if by magic. Fairatella greeted her cheerfully.

"Hello, Chosen One, no time for chit chat, hop on, grab the invisible reigns, prepare yourself for a bumpy ride!" said Eleganza, hovering as she spoke. Fairatella did as she asked, taking care not to get hit by her large wings that flapped rapidly. Puzzled about the reigns, she was still looking for them when out of nowhere, Mr. Mumble Bee appeared. He made a beeline for her, till he was right in her face, and almost sat on her nose. Fairatella, astonished, said, "What are you doing here?" She flicked him away with her hand as she spoke.

He answered in a mumbled voice; he always talked nasally. "I'm here for the ride!" He buzzed right back on to her nose.

"But you're not invited!" Fairatella said, irritated by his persistence.

"Am so. I'm, one of Serena's messengers too, so there!" Mr. Mumble Bee said whilst snuffing a lot.

"You are?" Fairatella said, taken by surprise. "Fine, if you insist," she huffed, and didn't look too happy about it. She thought it strange to have imagined someone who became real. *Serena's doing, no doubt.* Mr. Mumble Bee showed her where the reigns were.

Eleganza said, "Hold on tight, let's go, it's time you met your fairy godmother." Then she whispered, "She lives in the Forest of All-Seeing Eyes."

She flew with such speed it made Fairatella giddy, and Mr. Mumble Bee tried his best to keep up with them with his short, choppy wing strokes. Milky Brooks by night, compared to daytime, was as different as chalk and cheese; she wasn't used to staying up so late, and she saw places she never even knew existed, and even familiar places appeared different by the light of the moon. Enchanted by everything around her, she thought, *It's a magical night.* As she looked up at the star-studded sky, her head was thrust backwards, almost throwing her off balance. As she jolted back and forth, she saw a shooting star, which appeared to be falling in the same direction they were heading for. "Lucky star, make a wish," she hollered, and so she did, but kept her wish secret.

Eleganza said, "Shhh, a safe journey for us is what I wish!"

Mr. Mumble Bee heard from a distance, still lagging behind despite his furious flapping, and moaned, "I wish I was younger." He was finding it hard to keep up with them. He was a hefty little bug; it was surprising that he had managed to stay airborne for so long.

The star and the moon lit their way as they ventured far into the night; the landscape altered, and the unknown seemed menacing. Strange shadows took form beneath her, playing tricks on her mind, as they swiftly flew over the mysterious landscape. Eleganza started to lose momentum rather bumpily, as if she'd put on the breaks abruptly. Fairatella gasped when they finally slowed down; before them stood dark, tall trees.

*Eerie*, she thought as she shuddered.

"Behold, the Forest of All-Seeing Eyes," said Eleganza, relieved they'd arrived safely and in one piece.

# CHAPTER NINE

## *The Portal Tree*

Fairatella sensed that she was being watched; she gaped, rubbed her eyes, then opened them, wondering if she was hallucinating. She'd been held captive by thousands upon thousands of peculiar tree eyes, glaring, staring, blinking, twitching and squinting; she couldn't believe her own eyes. It was surreal, for sure. It was the weirdest experience she'd ever had, and it totally gave her the creeps, and her goose bumps were proof of that.

Mr. Mumble Bee appeared out of nowhere and, within an inch of her nose, gazed at her and said, "Boo! Bizzzarre, ain't it? Don't be afraid, they won't harm us."

She was just about to smack him on his nose when Eleganza whispered as she hovered:

"Dense forest of the day, be enchanted by night
Warden of the forest, behold, let there be light
Poof, portal appears, poof, veil disappears from sight."

All at once, the veil of darkness was drawn like a curtain, revealing a welcoming portal; she found herself drawn to its intense light. They approached slowly, and the portal burst with an array of flowers, and sweet jasmine hung in the night air, her favourite aroma. She looked back and saw that the veil of darkness had closed behind her. Unafraid, onwards she looked; she knew she was in the presence of goodness as she felt warmth and a tingly sensation overcome her.

Straight ahead, she caught sight of an old rowan tree with a vibrant display of red berries, which she thought was very unusual as it wasn't autumn yet. She knew that the colour red was deemed to be the best protection against enchantment, so that surely contributed to the rowan's protective abilities. Fairies considered the rowan tree sacred for apotropaically warding off witches and protecting them from evil witchcraft and enchantment, they also believed it to be a portal tree, a doorway into another world, offering you a chance to go somewhere and leave somewhere.

After noticing that the wrinkled old tree trunk had a red, tiny door, she wondered if Serena actually lived inside the tree hollow. She jumped off Eleganza's back and stood before the door, assuming that she had to knock or that a key would miraculously appear before her. She heard Eleganza whisper a rhyme:

"Open tiny door
I'm a friend not foe
It's good not evil
That awaits thy call."

By magic, the tiny door opened. Eleganza then said, "You must enter alone. I shall be waiting for you here, to take you safely home. I am far too big, I cannot fit through the door." She smiled at her reassuringly.

Mr. Mumble Bee buzzed, "Buzz, I can!" He perched himself on her shoulder.

Eleganza said, "Follow the fairy lights."

Fairatella crawled into the hollow, and she wondered if she'd fit. She did, and as Eleganza helped her by giving her a push, and then Fairatella elbowed her way through. She found herself inside what seemed to be a narrow passageway. How did I get inside here? she asked herself. *There's not enough room to swing a cat in here,* she thought, looking around her, but as she looked ahead, she realised that she was inside a long corridor at the end of which she could see a brightly lit room. Fairy lights were hanging from the ceiling above, all the way down the corridor. "Hmm, follow the fairy lights, said Eleganza." So, she did.

As she went further down the corridor, it widened so she could stand up, and the ceiling got higher too. Whilst she walked along, she found it hard to believe that she was actually inside a tree trunk, especially with the corridor being so long. She concluded that the rowan tree must be a portal after all. All the time, Mr. Mumble Bee was right beside her, humming in her ear, which she found annoying, but she was glad of his company.

"Humhumhum. Honey, honey, ha, ha, honey, la, la..." buzzed Mr. Mumble Bee. He was in a jolly old mood; he couldn't wait to see Fairatella's face when she finally saw Serena.

# CHAPTER TEN

## *Serena*

On approaching the bright room, Fairatella could see that the brilliant illumination consisted of thousands of fairy lights; it looked like Christmas time, but to her surprise they were flying around her fairy godmother like a whirlwind, but not as fast. She also noticed tiny firecrackers exploding everywhere and that the room was swarming with fireflies, but Serena was the brightest light source of them all. At last, she was face to face with her fairy godmother. Entranced by her beauty, and speechless, Fairatella just curtsied before her.

In a sweet voice, Serena said, "Rise Fairatella, the Chosen One." She came closer to greet Fairatella, holding out her hand in friendship, and in her other hand she held a Roman candle-like wand. She moved with such grace and oozed serenity. As their hands touched, Fairatella could feel that she was being charged by her warmth and energy, which completely calmed her and made her feel safe.

Fairatella gazed in awe at Serena and saw that she beamed, her eyes glowed with goodness, and she had a sugary smile. But it was the shooting star under her right eye that caught Fairatella's eye, as it shimmered as it streaked down onto her cheek and looked like a falling tear. She thought it strange as it appeared to be constantly on the go. *Serena shines like a star, too... Serena was that shooting star!* she thought.

Serena broke her train of thought by offering her refreshment, and she gladly accepted, Serena sipped a little, very elegantly, and said, "My daily dosage of happiness, three times a day, never fails."

Fairatella thought, *She has sugary manners too,* and replied, "So gracious of you, thank you."

"To happiness," said Serena, raising her goblet, and Fairatella did and said the same. They both sipped a little dose, and as their eyes fixed on one another, Fairatella became a bit anxious and looked at her with dismay.

*Golly gosh, now I must tell her why I'm here, what should I ask her first... if she can help me? Can she undo the spell, so I can lose this darn tail? Or can she help prevent Freakadella from making Tivarnia a land of misfits? Or perhaps I should just start with the forget-me-not borders?*

*Does she have the power to release the spell, so fairies can venture further than before and visit Earthlings, so they can believe in us again? Oh, and why am I being called the Chosen One? Oh dear, she'll think I'm talking gibberish, If I ask her so many questions. I'm in a muddle,* thought Fairatella, and sighed.

"Questions, questions, muddle indeed, no need, that puddle you're in is knee deep, just leap and be free!" said Serena, and gave her a smile of understanding.

*Leap?* thought Fairatella, then it clicked. Serena had read her thoughts. *Typical, telepathic, I should've known,* she thought, and felt a twinge of embarrassment. On second thought, she felt relieved as she no longer had to explain her problem; she'd already spilt the beans. "I'm such a fairy fool," Fairatella said, cross with herself.

Mr. Mumble Bee showed his face and said, "What's this about a muddle?" Then he turned towards Serena after he realised he'd forgotten his manners, and bowed before her and mumbled, "Your humble servant awaits your request, your highness." He turned back to Fairatella and said, "Don't bumble things up!"

Fairatella gave him a displeased look and snapped at him, "Look who's talking, Mr. Mumble Bumble!"

"No fool are you, fairy teller of tales, my heart warms to be in the presence of one so young yet so brave," said Serena, interrupting them.

Fairatella looked at Mr. Mumble Bee, then at Serena, and thought, *She means me? Me brave?* She gave a, so-there look to Mr. Mumble Bee.

"I've always watched over you. I could only reveal myself when the time was right," said Serena, capturing Fairatella's attention.

"Huh, right time?" replied Fairatella inquisitively.

"You had to seek me out first, to learn of your past, and now the time is ripe," said Serena, and Fairatella just nodded.

"We share a special bond," said Serena. She explained to her how she was the one who had interrupted Freakadella whilst she was chanting a spell for her mother Bellarosea, and what happened that day.

Serena looked at her serenely and said, "Only you can redeem us of this scourge that Freakadella has cast upon us, as it all started with you, the day she cursed you, before you were even born. You were the first misfit. Fate chose you, Chosen One."

"But how on earth am I supposed to do that?" Fairatella answered, looking baffled.

"Your heart is pure, and so The Lake of All Whispering Secrets, will whisper to you all you need to know, hopefully. I can only guide you," said Serena.

"What is this Whispering Lake? The Lake of All Whispering Secrets, did you say?" Fairatella asked.

Serena answered calmly, "It is a sacred place, a sanctuary for truth. Secrets are whispered to those who seek answers regarding themselves and their pasts, and the truth reveals itself. It is possible to hear the secrets of others, too, but only if they are directly connected to you; your secrets intertwine in a special way, and the lake allows it. Since your heart is pure, I have faith in you, and that you will hear secrets that will help you put an end to Freakadella's witchcraft."

Her eyes glittered as she spoke; she was so mellifluous that Fairatella listened to her voice with rapture and never doubted a single word she said. She nodded obediently.

"Once you have this knowledge, only then will you be ready to confront Freakadella," said Serena firmly.

"I understand, but where is the lake to be found, and the whereabouts of Freakadella's hideout?" said Fairatella, feeling overwhelmed and doubting that she was up to the daunting task that awaited her.

Serena replied, "Do not fear, Eleganza will take you to The Lake of All Whispering Secrets, but listen well, as it is wise that you, too, know of its whereabouts. Far from Milky Brooks, far beyond Yellow Meadows, over Bluebell Banks, through Poppy Valley to the distant Shady Land. Follow the Black River until you reach Misty Woods. Deep in the heart of the woods lies the lake. The river leads to the lake, but you must be on the right side, going north, as to the left of the lake lives Freakadella in her personal witch domain, Dark Hollows. Remember, you must get there before nightfall and be ready for the witching hour, when moonbeams first fall on the lake and fairy lights start to dance bewitchingly; this is the time secrets can be whispered and heard. Listen carefully, and with an open mind. The truth can be blinding, and you may fail at your task if you are judgmental."

Perplexed by everything she'd heard, Fairatella thought Serena was talking in riddles and that she had posed a conundrum, but still, she tried to remember her exact words, which she was good at, so she could try to make sense of it all later. She nodded and said she'd understood so far.

Serena gave her a reassuring smile and said, "It will all make sense when the time comes."

Realising she'd forgotten Serena's telepathic abilities with being slightly confused, Fairatella replied, "I hope so." She thought, *It's useless to pretend, she can see right through me,* and gave her an enigmatic smile.

Serena continued, "Once you have been bestowed with the knowledge that only the secrets whispered can provide you, you can then seek out Freakadella in Dark Hollows. In need, you can take refuge and rest on the tiny fairy isle, which is situated in the middle of the lake; a mysterious mist shields it from Freakadella's evil eye. If you half close your eyes, the mist forms a dragon shape, with outspread wings, and coincidently Freakadella happens to love dragons. It is best to rest and start off early in the morning, with the early bird's call. Freakadella sleeps most of the day; fortunately, you will arrive at her lair before she awakes. Follow the trail behind the fairy isle, and it will lead you to the Black River again, but don't be surprised if it is a blood-red river, as it just might be flowing with the blood of Freakadella's victims."

Fairatella gulped and her eyes rolled and became all goggle-eyed.

Serena explained to her about the stepping stones. "You must then cross the rushing river by the stepping stones;

due to an invisible force field hanging above them, you must keep low. Also, Freakadella has bewitched the stones, so cross cautiously, and you can only step on each stone once. If you fail, you will be bound to the stone until she can take you captive."

*Captive?* thought Fairatella, shaking her head; she got a little frightened.

Serena continued, "At this point, it's easy to be intercepted by Freakadella's messengers, so have your eyes open at all times. Be brave, as on the other side of the river the looming trees shroud the landscape in darkness, so proceed with caution as you are approaching her lair. Follow the riverbank upstream and soon you will come to an old stone bridge. Freakadella calls it Stonebridge, and it bridges a bloody bog, so be careful where you tread... it's better to just fly over!"

Fairatella knew she was concealing something from her, but she didn't dare to ask.

Serena then said, "Once you've crossed the bridge there is no turning back and remember she can smell your presence. Also, her messengers the three black crows will inform her of your arrival on sight of you. You will see what looks like a wishing well; the crows usually guard it, but don't be fooled, as it is a trap. Freakadella lives down that well." She laughed quietly a little and said, "That's the only place for her, actually, as she is too freaky and ugly for the light of day!"

Fairatella shuddered and gasped when she recalled her premonition about falling down a well and almost blasphemed, but she composed herself and tried to look brave. On seeing that she had turned ashen and looked troubled, Serena avoided telling her that the well led to an underground cavern, which one could get lost in, or of Freakadella's pet dragon Puffin, whom she had stolen from its mother Drakess, or of Batty and Battier. She thought, *What she doesn't know can't harm her, and besides, she might not have to venture deep into the cavern, or ever have to confront Drakess.* Serena hadn't foreseen the future this time; she knew there was no flying from fate, but she felt it in her bones that Fairatella would succeed in accomplishing her task as the Chosen One.

"I have told you all that you need to know. You have the presence of mind and you are now ready to oppose Freakadella and her dark magic. May the sacred elements guide you, your inner light glow bright and your energy be more powerful than ever before. Find the star inside you. Remember to always have fairy faith and to believe in yourself. It's a heavy burden to bear for such small shoulders, but you are strong, and Tivarnia will shine once again because of you. By the light and wisdom that our elders bestowed on us, I give you this wishing star," Serena said, then placed what looked like a stone carved star in the palm of Fairatella's hand and whispered something.

Fairatella looked at it in bewilderment and said, "Wishing star?" It started to glow dimly at first. On closer inspection she noticed it had strange markings engraved on it and wondered if it was an ancient fairy script or a stellar code of some kind. It glowed brighter the longer she held it, and she thought, *Wow, this is really cool.* She put it in her poppy pouch, closed her pouch, then took a peep at it and smiled when she saw that it no longer glowed; it was just a greyish stone.

Serena continued, "As you are already aware, fairies can't grant wishes for themselves, but with this wishing star, you can make a wish if it is for the good of others, an unselfish wish, but remember, only once, so use it wisely. Hold it tight in the palm of your hand and then place it close to your heart and say, "Wishing star of olde, elders grant me my wish, I wish for..."

Fairatella nodded and looked impressed.

Serena said, "It is a fragment of a shooting star, forged by the elders. It can light your way in the dark, and in your hour of need; the star will know when that time is. Go now, make haste, as you must arrive home before dawn. Eleganza will make sure you arrive home safely and help you whenever needed, that applies for Mr. Mumble Bee, too; my humble messenger will always be by your side."

He appeared out of nowhere and gave Fairatella a cheesy grin again; she couldn't help but smile back. Then she thanked Serena for all that she had done for her and kissed her right hand respectfully. They bid one another goodbye.

"Farewell, Chosen One," said Serena.

"Farewell Serena, fairest of all fairy godmothers." Fairatella never looked back, and a tiny tear fell from her right eye. It looked like a shooting star.

Eleganza was waiting for her outside like she had said she would be when Fairatella climbed out of the tiny tree door. She sluggishly climbed onto her back. This time Mr. Mumble Bee thought he'd park and ride by sitting on Fairatella's shoulder, after first complaining he was feeling rather fatigued.

"Take me home Eleganza," was all Fairatella said. She seemed lost in thought and was silent on the journey home. Eleganza knew better than to try to make polite conversation, so she let her be, and even Mr. Mumble Bee didn't seem to be annoying her any more.

Her return night flight seemed dreamlike, unreal in her half-conscious state. *Like a moving brushstroke of darkness,* she thought. Eleganza flew so rapidly that the strangely amorphous landscape moved fast and fluidly before her eyes, blurring into oblivion; night sounds were incoherent. Before she could say star struck, she was home safe and sound. In the hushed stillness of the night, she heard the night owl. Her vision no longer blurred, she saw, The Tree That Was, her home. It seemed so welcoming. Everyone was sleeping soundly at this late hour.

Eleganza hovered outside her bedroom window until Fairatella managed to climb through it, then whispered, "Meet me tomorrow, not too soon... late afternoon at the Buttercup Spring in Poppy Valley so as not to arouse suspicion. I know it's not nearby, but it's really not wise to be seen together in the light of day. Until then, be safe and mention it to no one; goodnight."

Fairatella nodded and said, "I know the place, a fairy goodnight to you too, Eleganza."

Mr. Mumble Bee appeared in front of her nose and pretended he was already asleep and snored, "ZZZZzzzzZZZZzzzz." Fairatella stifled a laugh by covering her mouth with one hand, and waved goodbye with the other.

She crept onto her feather bed and stretched out like a cat silently, so as not to wake Daisy. She lay there for a while, motionless, and although she was exhausted her head was still buzzing, and she couldn't sleep a wink. The ceiling of her bedroom was dome-shaped, with star cut holes for Earthlings to see the candle burning from within, but she gazed out to see the night sky, her very own skylight which she called her Stardome. She counted stars until she fell fast asleep.

# CHAPTER ELEVEN

## *Fairyitis*

Daisy climbed onto Fairatella's Wurlitzer feather bed rather clumsily and fell on top of her, then tried to sidle up next to her, but she didn't wake up, she just tossed about in her sleep some more. *Strange,* thought Daisy, thinking that she should've woken with a start, so she desperately tried to spin the bed around using her feet and arms to wake her. She just about managed to twirl the bed slowly round and round, but still Fairatella didn't wake up.

Puzzled, she thought she'd better take more extreme measures, so she spoke loudly in her ear, "Wakey, wakey sunshine." Fairatella momentarily raised an eyelid and looked at her out of the corner of her eye; the other eye remained shut. Then she slipped back into her coma.

Impatiently, Daisy shouted in Fairatella's ear, "No breakfast today?" which startled her a little.

Fairatella replied, "What's all the fuss about!" and buried her head in her pillow.

Daisy jumped off the bed, and with all her might started to spin the bed as fast as she could and shouted, "I'm hungry!"

"Oh no, my head's spinning, I must have drunk too much fairy punch last night," Fairatella said, in a frail voice.

Daisy giggled.

Now in the land of the living, Fairatella realised her dizziness was due to Daisy spinning her and said, "You're up early for a change."

Daisy shook her head and said, "Nope, it's very late. I've been ordered to wake you, so you can make us all breakfast."

Still feeling tired, Fairatella thought the idea of having to do chores all day was daunting, and besides, she needed to build up her strength for her task, so she decided to pretend to be ill, that way she could stay in bed.

"Tell Alexmeania I'm sick, I must have drunk or eaten something at the party that doesn't agree with me, I can't get up, see!" moaned Fairatella, and she faked fainting and looked sickly and said, "I might not survive."

Daisy looked concerned, then shot off. Slightly alarmed, Fairatella realised she'd better think of something quick before Alexmeania came to check up on her, something convincing, as she was no fool. She racked her brains for ideas for her supposed sickness until she had a flash of genius. On her windowsill were forget-me-nots in a vase, what she also called the 'itchy flower', so she grabbed them and rubbed her chest and arms with them. She was aware that the flower could induce an adverse skin reaction, including itching, and even a rash, as she had had one before, but since her last rash had appeared a while after contact, she thought she'd better speed things up a bit, so she scratched herself erratically until a rash appeared. Then she jumped back into bed and covered herself with the sheets.

Fairatella pretended to be asleep when Alexmeania entered the bedroom, already looking suspicious; she stormed up to her bed and nudged her and, as Fairatella did not respond, she nipped her on her cheek. Slowly lifting her eyelids, Fairatella just looked at her pathetically like a loyal dog.

"So, you've been stricken dumb by this mysterious illness of yours, eh?" said Alexmeania.

Fairatella nodded as if she was in pain. Not at all convinced, Alexmeania grabbed the sheets off her with disbelief, and she was completely taken by surprise when she saw the rash. Fairatella beckoned her to come closer so she could whisper something in her ear; Alexmeania approached cautiously lending Fairatella her ear.

Pretending she was almost choking, Fairatella said, "Con-ta-gious."

Panic-stricken, Alexmeania jumped backwards and stumbled. Lost for words, she started to itch and scratch a little. Deep in thought, she glared at Fairatella whilst she nibbled at her fingernails. She looked at her chewed nails, then felt disgusted with herself for nibbling them, thinking she might very well have caught some mysterious Fairyitis disease in doing so.

"To avoid an epidemic you're in quarantine," Alexmeania said hastily, and made a hurried departure, slamming the door behind her. Then she shouted "Daisy!" at the top of her voice. "Don't go near that unhealthy fairy!"

Daisy in the meantime had been hiding under her bed. Fairatella spotted her and saw that she was scared, so she winked at her and signalled for her to come closer. Surprised, and not sure whether to be relieved or not, Daisy approached Fairatella, taking little steps, and said, "But aren't you sick? I might catch it!"

"Codswallop, can you keep a secret?" said Fairatella.

Daisy's eyes lit up and she replied, "I love secrets," and nodded emphatically.

"I'm not really sick, just tired, and I don't want to be doing chores all day," said Fairatella, and smiled. She explained about the itchy flower. "Go and play now, remember not to tell a fairy soul about our secret."

Daisy agreed and left the room, skipping happily.

"Alone at last! I can relax," said Fairatella, and she did. She was satisfied with herself for tricking Alexmeania, but after a while she became uneasy. With a sense of foreboding she recalled the task that awaited her. *If I'm the Chosen One*, she thought, *I have to at least try. This is no time for being weak willed.* She pulled herself together, popped a poppy seed and thought of a plan as she lay sprawled out on the bed. Contemplating what she had to do next, she said to herself out loud, "Hmm, Eleganza said I had to meet her in Poppy Valley in the early afternoon, it would be difficult for me to sneak out of the house before dark, too. Now let me see... hmm, I need an excuse to get away without arousing any suspicion, and I'm supposed to be sick, so..."

Her thoughts were interrupted by voices coming from below; from what she could make out, someone had come to call on them unexpectedly. Curious to see who the visitor was, she went to look out of her bedroom window, but the visitor wasn't visible, so she tried to eavesdrop and almost fell out of the window in doing so. To her surprise, it sounded like Azaar. *It can't be,* she thought.

"I've come to return Fairatella's purse, she dropped it as she was leaving my party last night," said Azaar.

Fairatella overhead what he said and realised it actually was him. She was taken aback and accidently knocked over the vase with the forget-me-nots from her windowsill. It almost hit Azaar on his head as it fell, but he ducked just in time. He looked up but, as he saw no one, he scratched his head, shrugged his shoulders and carried on talking. Fairatella got into such a spin that she felt faint and almost lost her bearings whilst in search of her bed.

When she eventually stumbled on to her bed, she was a little flustered. Not being able to think straight, she squeezed her head with her hands and said, "Oh no, well isn't this just dandy, he couldn't have chosen a worse time to call! Now what am I going to do?"

Suddenly, Alexmeania barged in on her, all excited, and said, "You'll never guess who's come to call?"

"Don't tell me, Prince Charming?" Fairatella replied sarcastically.

Alexmeania nodded her head in agreement and said, "How did you guess... well, pretty close, it's Azaar!" She was hardly able to contain her delight; she waited for Fairatella's response, thinking that she'd be overjoyed too.

Instead Fairatella looked at her with a blank expression and dampened her enthusiasm by shouting, "Lucky little me, tell him to go away, I'm sick!"

Bewildered, Alexmeania thought that Fairatella must be slightly touched in the head due to a strange fever or other symptoms of her ailment and tried to coerce her into seeing Azaar.

"But it's THE AZAAR, I told him you weren't feeling well but he insisted that he gave back your purse himself personally, such a darling," said Alexmeania.

Fairatella had to get rid of Azaar once and for all, and she thought she knew how. Fairatella squinted her eyes on purpose and said, "We wouldn't want darling Azaar to catch my illness, too, would we now?"

Alexmeania had to think about that for a little while, as she didn't want to miss a perfect opportunity, Azaar being so popular and all, she even imagined herself being his mother-in-law. She looked relieved when an idea came to her.

"What if it's outside in the open air, surely he won't catch it then?" said Alexmeania.

Stupefied, Fairatella just lay there and gaped at her.

Alexmeania realised she'd not yet convinced her, so she continued improvising and said, "Perhaps a walk then, it's a lovely day outside?"

*That woman has lost her marbles,* thought Fairatella, and was just about to say, *But I'm sick, and I'm bed ridden, how can I walk?* when she had a brainwave. It occurred to her that Alexmeania had just given her the excuse she'd been looking for all along. *What a fluke of luck,* she thought. She sat up in bed and said, "A walk, yes, just what I need." She looked at her arms and chest and pretended to look surprised and said, "Oh, what a coincidence, the rash has gone!" Jumping out of bed with newly found energy, she shouted, "In fact, I'm as fit as a fiddle!"

Normally, Alexmeania would've been suspicious of her miraculous recovery, but that day, her desire to be popular blinded all her suspicions and she was too easily fooled. She gave a sigh of relief and thought, *Thank goodness, she's finally come to her senses.*

"I'll just freshen up and I'll be down in five," said Fairatella. She wanted to buy time, as she had to prepare for the task ahead, and she had to take whatever she needed with her, as she wouldn't be returning home after the walk with Azaar.

"Don't keep Azaar waiting too long," Alexmeania said cheerfully as she left the room; she was eager to tell Azaar that Fairatella was well enough after all.

Whilst sitting for a moment, Fairatella composed herself and quickly thought of a plan: "I could walk through Yellow Meadows and over the Bluebell Banks with him and think of an excuse later as to why I should continue alone to Poppy Valley to meet Eleganza, without him suspecting anything." Whilst she thought about what to take with her, Mr. Mumble Bee appeared out of nowhere, looking distraught. Apparently, he had beefriended Pan, the tadpole and he was worried that the big nasty Koi carp, Scar Fish Face, who also resided in the pond next door, might eat Pan whilst Fairatella was gone. Pan had upset Scar Fish Face by calling him a buffoon.

"Enough of your buffoonery, Mr. Mumble Bee, I can't be thinking about Pan at a time like this! You don't really expect me to take him with me?" said Fairatella, exasperated.

Mr. Mumble Bee looked at her pitifully and begged her, "Pleazzzz, don't you want him, to be safe? If he gets eaten, who would tickle your toes?"

Fairatella raised her eyebrows and said, "Oh, very well," realising the danger he might be in and that he really was a good friend of hers. "But how am I supposed to carry him? He'd be like a fish out of water!"

Mr. Mumble Bee grinned on seeing an empty glass jar on Fairatella's dressing table and buzzed over to it and said, "Perfect! Fill it with water and he'll be fine."

Fairatella agreed and said, "Very well, now you must excuse me Mr. Mumble Bee, I have things to do."

He smiled his gratitude to her and then vanished into thin air.

As fast as she could, Fairatella got ready; she found her poppy pouch, checked to see if the wishing star was still inside and that her pixie dust was still in the inside pocket. She sprinkled a little of the dust over Daisy's bed and wished that she'd be safe until she returned, then closed her pouch tight. She needed something for the glass jar, to carry it better, and found some string, wrapped it around the lip of the jar and made a handle to hold. Putting on her boots, she noticed her tail, so she stood up and grabbed for it. She was about to hide it but changed her mind and let it go free again. She was too anxious to care about what others thought of her tail; she took one last look around her bedroom and dashed off to greet Azaar.

When she entered the living room, Daisy was gulping down a fairy cake while Alexmeania was offering Azaar and Silver refreshment; feeling thirsty she snatched a glass too and drank it quickly in one gulp. Suddenly, as if stricken by pain, she touched her forehead with the back of her hand.

Alexmeania, horrified, thinking that she might be mentally deranged after all, helped her to sit down and said, "Do you have a splitting headache, dearest? Are you not feeling well again?"

Flexing her facial muscles and jaw, Fairatella said in a strained voice, "Brain freeze!"

Everyone looked at her with doubt, wondering if she'd gone mad or not, except Azaar, who wasn't sure if he should take her seriously or not, and found her adorably potty.

"Ice tea, so icy, frooooozen, brain freeze. Get it?" Fairatella said whilst her teeth chattered.

Daisy nodded and giggled. Then, suddenly, she frowned a little and said, "Is it contagious Fairatella?"

Relieved to see her able to talk again, Alexmeania heaved a sigh of relief and signalled for her to approach Azaar, without delay.

Silver shook his head in disapproval, at Alexmeania's relentless determination, to match-make Fairatella and

Azaar. "In her own good time Alexmeania, give her a chance to recover first!" said Silver and smiled at Fairatella. After she came around, Fairatella stood up and went to greet Azaar and apologised for keeping him waiting.

"That's quite all right. I'm glad to see that you are well again." He handed her the purse. "You dropped it last night when you were in a hurry to leave," said Azaar.

"Oh, so kind of you," said Fairatella. She put the purse down on the nearest table and said, "Shall we go for that walk now?" She was eager to get away and was feeling a little awkward too.

"If you're sure you're feeling up to it?" said Azaar.

Fairatella nodded and said in a chirpy voice, "I've never felt better!"

She fondly kissed her father on the forehead and hugged him silently, in a way she hadn't done before, and he sensed that something was bothering her, so he held her tight, hoping it would make her feel better. It wasn't easy for Fairatella to be so secretive, especially with her father, whom she was close to. They didn't have any secrets and they could talk about anything and everything. She picked up Daisy and hugged her warmly, as if it would be for the last time, and hoped she would be safe until she returned. If she ever did return, she thought sadly, but she told herself to think positive. Daisy touched Fairatella's head to see if it was still frozen, as she thought she was acting very strangely. Fairatella just gave her a loving smile, as she was stuck for words. She saw that Alexmeania was looking at her and Daisy, Alexmeania gave a jealous glance, Fairatella was aware that she envied her sisterly bond with Daisy and thought, *It wouldn't bother me at all, if I never saw that mean Alexmeania ever again.* She bade them all goodbye, and so did Azaar.

Azaar raised his hand, indicating the way out, and said, "After you."

Upon leaving, Fairatella took one last look over her shoulder at her father, Daisy and The Tree That Was, and hoped it wasn't for the last time. She fixed the image of them in the forefront of her mind, so she could recall it easily.

Already feeling quite nostalgic, she almost forgot about Pan and rushed over to the pond next door; nothing seemed to be out of the ordinary, and there were no signs of the big nasty, Koi carp, Scar Fish Face. She knelt beside the pond and looked for Pan. On spotting him, she scooped him up, with the glass jar and filled it to just below the brim with pond water.

Pan shouted, "Help, I'm being kidnapped!"

Fairatella put her face up close to the jar; her nose looked squashed, as she'd pressed it against the glass, and her eyes looked magnified through the glass. She stared at him.

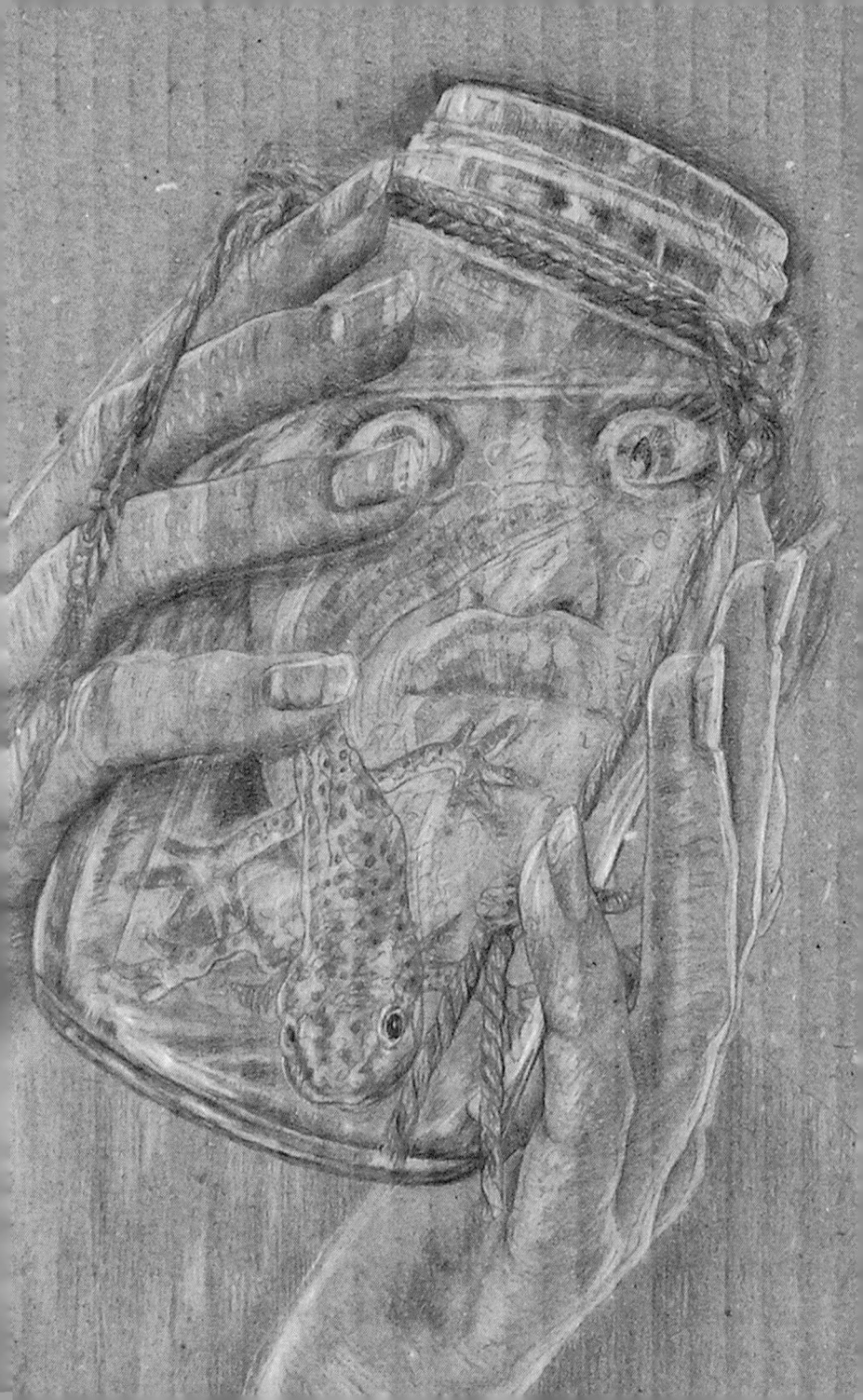

Pan, relieved, said, "Oh, it's you, are you insane? You scared the living daylights out of me!"

In the meantime, Azaar had followed Fairatella and was observing what she was doing; he was beginning to think perhaps she really was nuts. He interrupted and said, "Fairatella, is everything all right? Err, would you prefer it if we went fishing?"

Fairatella was taken by surprise, as she'd forgotten he was there. She looked quickly over her shoulder at him and spilt some of the water from the glass jar; Pan was tossed about like he was at sea. On seeing that, Azaar looked concerned for her sanity. It amused her, and she thought she could play on it. *I could easily get rid of him this way,* she thought.

She smiled at him like a nitwit and said, "No, I'd prefer to walk, and we can bring Pan with us, you don't mind, do you?"

Azaar awkwardly replied, "So, you often go for walks with tadpoles, do you?"

Giggling to herself, she thought, *He thinks I'm a lunatic, ha!* and then said, "Oh yeah, Pan and I always go for walks together, we're inseparable."

At this point, Pan was completely baffled and said, "A walk?"

"Shhh," replied Fairatella, and whispered to him, "You'll give me away. I'll explain later. Everything will be OK, I promise."

Pan shook his head and whispered back, "I doubt that; put me back in the pond now or I'll scream!"

Fairatella, exasperated, said, "But I'm rescuing you from that nasty Scar Fish Face." Before Pan had the time to answer, she turned around and looked at Azaar straight in the eye and said, "Shall we go? I love the Yellow Meadows, let's go for a stroll there."

She covered the jar with her hand, drowning out Pan's voice. He was frantically swimming around and shouted, "But, but, but, I protest!"

Azaar, not sure what to make of the situation, just agreed and said, "Yellow Meadows it is, then."

Off they both walked towards the meadows, side by side, Fairatella holding Pan. Every now and then, she'd look at Pan adoringly, pampering him with sweet words.

"Oh, just look at him, isn't he just the cutest little tadpole you've ever set eyes on!" Fairatella said, whilst she stroked the jar. After she took a few more steps then said, "Lucky little Pan, having his very own portable aquarium."

Azaar thought that she was acting peculiar, but brushed it off, putting it down to nerves; after all, it was their first date and he usually did have that effect on his girlfriends.

# CHAPTER TWELVE

## Dandelion Wish

Time elapsed smoothly as they made light conversation, and before they knew it, they were strolling through the meadows, quite at ease. It was a lovely afternoon; the country air was refreshing and being surrounded by the beauty of nature made them feel carefree. Even Pan seemed content, and he felt quite adventurous, meandering through the meadows, seeing places for the first time.

The further they ventured, the more at ease they felt with one another. Azaar made her laugh. *He's quite entertaining, I never expected to enjoy his company so much,* she thought. Fairatella was so absorbed in conversation with Azaar, that she forgot all about her task ahead, until he suddenly changed the subject.

"So, what's this about you acting all crazy? Care to enlighten me, I'm really intrigued as to why?" said Azaar.

He almost startled her by ambushing her so unexpectedly; she hadn't realised that he was so intelligent and thought, *He must have been playing with me, all this time—unbelievable—I've been spoofed!* Not wanting to show her surprise, she snapped off a dandelion stalk, then blew the dandelion in his face. The spores tangled with his hair, and she chuckled a little. She pretended that she hadn't understood him and said, "I have no idea what you're talking about; me, crazy?" whilst blowing another dandelion. The spores floated away with the wind.

"Fine, be mysterious," said Azaar, smiling, but really, he was feeling slightly peeved because she wouldn't open up to him. He tried to hide his feelings by changing the subject and said, "You didn't make a wish."

"A wish?" said Fairatella, raising her eyebrows.

"That's what one does after blowing a dandelion," said Azaar, and winked at her.

Fairatella answered, "Aha, OK, I wish for..." She secretly wished that she would see him again.

"Hmm, I like secretive and mysterious fairies," said Azaar, flashing a big white smile at her. "Mischievous too!"

Fairatella answered, "Do you now!"

They carried on ambling through the meadows. Shortly after, they found themselves walking along Bluebell Banks, and Azaar enquired if perhaps they should be getting back.

"Oh no, I'm enjoying myself too much, this is one of my favourite places! Besides, I won't be missed," said Fairatella, after thinking that she needed him to take her up to Poppy Valley at least, so by the time he returned home, she will be long gone, and no one would be able to find her.

He indulged her every whim, eager to win her favour, and he agreed to continue as long as she wanted.

"I didn't want you to get into any trouble on my behalf, that's all," said Azaar.

"Trouble? Nah, fiddlesticks, Alexmeania is over the moon that I'm out walking with you. In fact, I bet she's nibbling everything in sight right now, anxious to learn if we hit it off or not!" said Fairatella.

Azaar grinned and said humorously, "Weird fairy, that Alexmeania, I've never seen a fairy nibble so much before. She made me feel anxious just by watching her; I was compelled to nibble my nails, too, but instead I just nibbled at a celery stick to stop the urge of chewing off all my nails." He looked at his neat nails admiringly and said, "I take such good care of them usually, it would've been such a pity."

Fairatella convulsed with laughter. Azaar was happy to be winning her over.

"Last night you made me smile, and Daisy laughed so much that she had belly ache. Tulipa's face was a picture after that illusion trick you played on her. I never did get the opportunity to thank you for sticking up for me," said Fairatella.

"You are most welcome; she deserved it," said Azaar righteously.

"I think you went too far, though," said Fairatella, looking shame-faced.

"Oh, really?" replied Azaar.

Fairatella just gave him a little smile. He commented on what a captivating smile she had, and Fairatella bashfully said, "Flatterer." She was thinking how charming he was when she saw that they were approaching Poppy Valley. Fairatella thought, *This is no time to be swept off my feet; I still need to think of an excuse for leaving him behind without making him dubious.*

Out of the blue, Azaar said, "I'm glad I found your purse; fortune smiled on me, as it seems like fate willed us to be together. Your purse was empty when I picked it up, I hope you didn't lose anything valuable?"

Overjoyed, Fairatella said, "And fortune just smiled again!"

"Huh?" responded Azaar.

He had given her the excuse she'd been looking for; she popped a poppy seed, and he found her amusing.

"Yes! My poppy seeds are very valuable, indeed. They must have fallen out, when I dropped my purse. Now I'm short on seeds, and I need to stock up on my supply again. I say, since we're near Poppy Valley, would you mind terribly if I went to collect seeds... alone?" said Fairatella.

Azaar, surprised, said, "Alone? But I don't mind escorting you there."

Fairatella answered, "Hmm, it's a secret place, so no one can accompany me there," and hoped she sounded convincing.

"I'm good at keeping secrets," he said sharp-wittedly.

"Ha-ha, so am I, that's why I can't reveal the spot. Believe me, you wouldn't like it there anyway. Besides, I prefer to be alone when collecting seeds, I find it therapeutic," said Fairatella. She hoped that he wouldn't get offended.

"Fine, have it your way," said Azaar. He did suspect that something was wrong; her strange behaviour was sufficient proof alone, but he knew she must have had a good reason for being so secretive, so he didn't press the matter any further and changed the subject.

"What's so special about poppy seeds, anyway? Most eat sugar-coated berries, pomegranate seeds, et cetera," said Azaar.

She realised he had understood that something was bothering her, and she appreciated him more for pretending not to have noticed, and answered, "Poppy seeds are not as fattening as sugary fruits, and they are a better source of minerals, and they have magical qualities too!"

"They must have!" said Azaar and laughed heartily.

She almost wished she could share her secret with him, to lighten her burden, but she'd promised not to. All this time, she'd forgotten about her tail; he had never even looked at it or mentioned it once, and she thought, *That's odd, perhaps I misjudged him after all.* Her tail drooped and wrapped around one of her ankles. They walked side by side. Azaar had the urge to hold her hand but he saw that her mind was elsewhere.

When they reached Poppy Valley, Fairatella said, "It's time for me to leave now," and held his gaze.

"It was fun, we should do it again sometime," said Azaar, hoping she'd agree to another outing.

"Are you sure? I am cursed, you know!" replied Fairatella, trying her best to impersonate a bad-tempered hellcat.

Azaar felt a little awkward; he didn't know what to make of her strange behaviour. He was stuck for words and just said, "Err..."

As soon as she saw his puzzled expression, Fairatella chuckled and said, "Joking!" She grinned at him and thought, *If only he really knew...*

Azaar gave a sigh of relief, which Fairatella thought was very funny. She enjoyed teasing him.

Fairatella shrugged her shoulders and said casually, "If fate wills it, we'll meet again; see you around Azaar."

She held the jar with Pan in tightly, with both hands. Azaar winked at her and she flew off before he had the chance to say goodbye. This time they parted as close friends; she hoped she'd see him again under better circumstances, but definitely not while she was still cursed! She looked back and saw he was still standing there; he raised his hand to wave. *Bye, charmer,* she thought, and then looked ahead.

Pan was afraid of heights, and he waved his hands at her and cried, "S.O.S!"

Fairatella replied reassuringly, "Be patient, Pan, we're nearly there."

As she flew swiftly, her mind repeated Serena's words over and over again. To prevent her stomach from turning, she tried to pop a seed, but she needed both her hands to hold Pan, so she just kept telling herself that she was ready for everything, until she believed that she was, and then said quietly, "So it begins..."

# CHAPTER THIRTEEN

## *The Lake of All Whispering Secrets*

On approaching Buttercup Spring, Fairatella said, "Nearly there now, Pan, hold on." She could see he was having another fit of dizziness; he was pale in the face and was just floating on his back. "I hope we're not late," she said, looking concerned.

"Late for what?" said Pan. His ears pricked up, and he came to after realising they were losing height. He hoped for a smooth landing and uttered, "Sink or swim," then held his breath.

"Soon, Pan, I'll be able to explain," said Fairatella. She regretted taking Pan with her and thought, *If I'd only known that he was afraid of heights and got giddy, I would have found another way to rescue him from the hands of nasty Scar Fish Face. What was I thinking? I acted without thinking, that's what. It's all that Mr. Mumble's fault, I should never have listened to that old buffoon.*

Mr. Mumble Bee appeared in front of her and almost collided with her.

Fairatella said, "Watch out, you nincompoop," spilling more water from the jar.

Mr. Mumble Bee realised he was out of favour again.

She didn't pay him any attention because she spotted Eleganza in the near distance, already waiting for her. All in a tiff, she said, in an apologetic tone as she landed, "Sorry, I hope I'm not too late?" Short of breath, she then greeted Eleganza properly as an afterthought, as she had almost forgot her manners. *I hope we can still make it in time,* she thought.

Eleganza was never impolite, but she had to be quick about greeting Fairatella and said, "If we delay further, we will miss the witching hour," anticipating her thought.

At the Buttercup Spring, Fairatella filled the jar with spring water, splashed some of the cool water onto her face, moistened her lips and tasted the spring water, and then drank some thirstily.

"No more time wasting, all aboard, we're bound for the Lake of All Whispering Secrets," said Eleganza hastily.

Fairatella hopped on as fast as she could; she found the invisible reigns, secured Pan on the hump of Eleganza's back and told Eleganza that flying made Pan feel sick.

"I know, I'll do my best to keep steady," said Eleganza.

Fairatella shouted, "Ready!"

The take-off was a little bumpy. Fairatella was used to it but Pan wasn't. She quickly explained to Pan as much as he needed to know, and without scaring him, she told him about the lake that whispered secrets and that she hoped to hear a whisper that could help her get rid of her tail, perhaps even release the spell and the spells put on all the other misfits, but she never mentioned anything about confronting Freakadella. After a while, she thought, *Strange, Eleganza never asked me what took me so long or why Pan was here; perhaps Mr. Mumble Bee already told her?* She looked back to see if Mr. Mumble Bee was still following, and he was, but he was struggling to keep up as usual.

So swiftly they flew that she no longer recognised her surroundings; they had already passed Poppy Valley and they were now flying over what must be Shady Land. She thought, *I can tell why they call it that.* She couldn't see the ground at all, as overlapping shadows shaded it. All kinds of strange shadows were being cast depending on the light, which was slowly starting to fade. These shadows played tricks on her mind, but she felt safe with Eleganza, and they were flying too high for her to feel threatened, but still she preferred not to look down.

Little did she know that those who had walked there before never returned home. If she had walked through the shadows of darkness, she most surely would've been afraid, as it is said that the shadows you fear the most follow you, and there is no escaping them until they have driven you insane.

Although they were travelling at a considerable speed of 45mph, it felt like 324mph. Eleganza flew steadily and Pan never complained; perhaps his silence was due to the fact that he wanted to help Fairatella find the solution to her problems.

She heard the sound of rushing water coming from below, so she looked down, and there she saw the Black River that Serena had described. It looked menacing, not only because of its colour but because of how the water raged relentlessly. Eleganza headed north and kept on the right side of the river as Serena had advised. She remembered everything Serena had said and wondered how long it would be before they approached the Misty Woods. What seemed like forever for the little tadpole was only a heartbeat for Fairatella.

The Misty Woods seemed to glower at her from a distance, and as they approached she observed that the shielding mist hung over the woods, as if to keep watch over the Misty Woods and hide it simultaneously. *From whom was the mist protecting the woods from? Surely not the likes of me... Someone wants to keep this place a secret, that's for sure,* thought Fairatella, and she felt nervous.

Eleganza slowed down as they entered the woods and hovered until Mr. Mumble Bee caught up with them. They proceeded with caution, and although they kept their eyes peeled, the mysterious mist made it difficult for them to see clearly. Fairatella remembered that the lake lay deep in the heart of the woods, and with the light slowly fading all around her, she couldn't help but wonder if they'd make it in time.

Eleganza said, after being silent the whole way, "We are nearly there now, do not fear, Chosen One."

Suddenly, Fairatella was thrown into the air, as Eleganza had been blind sighted by the mist, and she was over exerted too. Her wing had gotten caught on a broken tree branch, causing her to break abruptly. Luckily for Fairatella, she used her tail to regain her balance by wrapping it around a higher branch above her. She was still hanging upside down when she just about managed to grab Pan and the jar in time; he'd been thrown out of his jar and was panicking, gasping for breath. Very little pond water remained.

"I can fill it up again, Pan, with water from the lake," Fairatella said reassuringly. Even though she was shook up, she still had a clear head and sharp reflexes. Looking down at Eleganza, she could see that she'd been hurt, but Eleganza never uttered a word, as she didn't want to alarm Fairatella. Fairatella helped to release her diaphanous wing as fast as she could, cursing her luck as she did so.

"I hope you're not in any pain?" Fairatella said worriedly.

"I'll be fine. What's a scratch, for the sake of a free Tivarnia?" Eleganza said, inspiring her to be brave.

"Now what am I going to do?" asked Fairatella, thinking it might all be over.

"Continue alone, of course. I'll catch up with you later after I've rested for a while," said Eleganza.

Fairatella looked at her in dismay, then looked about her and uttered, "Alone? But I couldn't possibly..." The eerie woods spooked her a little.

Eleganza insisted that she should continue and said, "Only you can hear your secrets whispered anyway, and it's not that far now." She took short breaths as she tried to talk and said feebly, "Straight ahead of you, look yonder."

A long way away, Fairatella could just about see the lake through the mist; it was also screened by a row of trees standing close together. She wondered if the trees weren't only sheltering the lake from adverse weather, but keeping it from being seen, just like the mist.

"Go now, time is against us. I'll be all right," urged Eleganza.

Fairatella nodded emphatically, then she headed quickly towards the lake; she looked back at Eleganza only for an instant, as she didn't like leaving her, but there was nothing else she could do.

Mr. Mumble Bee appeared all at once and said, "She'll beeeee fine."

"I wish you wouldn't keep startling me like that," said Fairatella, trying to look annoyed, but really, she was glad to see him. Her wings then flapped vigorously; she swooped, and he couldn't keep up with her.

As the sun was almost setting, fading fire colours could be seen through the distant trees, and Fairatella said, "Soon it will be the witching hour."

She remembered Serena's words by heart: "When moonbeams first fall on the lake and fairy lights start to dance bewitchingly, this is the time secrets can be whispered and heard."

Panic-stricken, Fairatella gained speed, flying low or running depending on what obstacles she had in front of her; it was getting darker by the second. Holding tightly to Pan in his jar, and with Mr. Mumble Bee not far behind, she ventured forth desperately, as if her life depended on it and all of Tivarnia. Whilst she was running, she could hear her heart pounding, and she clasped her mother's locket for a moment; it was beating against her chest, but she had to hold Pan tightly. She sensed her mother was only an echo away and remembered that she always was, even in the dark, since their two hearts were bound by love. That gave her an inner strength that she'd never experienced before, and she almost heard her mother telling her she could do it, she was strong, and she became a fairy of light and energy.

"Always have fairy faith, believe in myself, that's what Serena said!" exclaimed Fairatella. She had prepared herself and was ready for everything.

Just in the nick of time, they arrived at the lakeside, and low and behold, just as her fairy godmother had foretold, she witnessed the witching hour. It was the most beautiful sight she'd ever seen: fairy lights dancing on the water's surface bewitchingly. Whilst catching her breath, her heart still pounding, she stood there in awe. After recovering for a short while, she remembered to fill Pan's jar with lake water and placed him down securely between some rocks at the water's edge. Upon closer inspection, she noticed that the fairy lights were actually fairies, the tiniest fairies she'd ever seen, all aglow, and some were like firecrackers. Others performed what she thought looked like glamorous, synchronised swimming and flying; she was absolutely mesmerised.

...ion of love, because it made her
...ne felt.

...ismay, she heard the strangest and
...of all, Freakadella's actual curse.
...l pay for this; so sweet will be my
...rnia will shudder!"

...ortified and thought, *This is some*
*...ot be true,* and rubbed her eyes in
*...g to go down well on my popularity*
*...wicked old witch is my aunt? How*
*...mother was a fairy and Freakadella*
*...ey were just step-sisters,* Fairatella

...tinued, but still none made sense to
...inner voice urged her to determine
...della's hatred; she hoped that would
...drum of entangled secrets. Nothing
...had led her to believe that it was
...who was to blame for their sisterly
...ary, she loved Freakadella and felt
...hat she couldn't find happiness; she
...to have incomparable beauty and
...fairy in Tivarnia. But then, Fairatella
...ration, which completely bowled her
...een filled with repulsion at the sight
...her ways too. He had tried to be
...t first, but she'd misinterpreted his
...clear as a bell, Fairatella heard her
...have no place here in Tivarnia,
...dn't believe that her father had

As the surface of the lake shimmered in the magical moonlight, the whispers began. Moonstruck, she thought it was the glittering moonbeams that were either capturing whispers or releasing them, or the fairy lights themselves were the whisperers; she didn't have the time to figure it out. She struggled to hear the whispers at first, as they sounded like mere echoes in the wind, and they seemed to be all jumbled up, which confused her considerably. "Clarity of thought is the key to understanding the secrets whispered, and for seeking truth," whispered Fairatella, and then she listened harder. Gradually, the whispers got louder, but she still could make no sense of them, as they seemed to overlap one another. She listened for her inner voice, and as she calmed in the stillness of meditation, she heard herself say, "Clarity can be found only by fully concentrating; put aside your personal thoughts, empty your mind and then listen carefully." The harder she concentrated, the clearer the whispers became, until she was like a sound barrier for sound waves and sonic vibrations. She had let herself become the vehicle that absorbed whispers, a receiver without being overcome by them. The whispers were fast and weird, but she tried channelling them, one at a time. After doing so, she tuned in to the most unbelievable secrets.

At first, she heard secrets that had been recently whispered, like her very own: how she hated her tail and would do anything to get rid of it, and how she wished to be like all other fairies. She also heard a secret of her father's that made her happy, because she learned that he

said such a thing; it was so unlike him and she wondered if he was to blame for Freakadella being ostracised.

Although Freakadella had been deeply hurt, she had never showed it. Over the course of time, she was consumed by bitterness, and bitterness led to maliciousness, which eventually turned into pure evil. With the passing of each day, she transformed into the freakiest witch ever; evil itself created her and was devouring her soul, little by little, piece by piece. Her fairy wings of light rapidly disintegrated in a dense darkness. Freakadella knew she would lose her wings forever, but she didn't mind at all. Not in the least, as she hated being a fairy.

All at once, Fairatella lost track of her thoughts when whispers came from further back in time, revealing that Freakadella had wished for harm to come to Bellarosea, so that her face would be badly disfigured, because she desperately wanted to be prettier than Bellarosea. *Well, that doesn't surprise me at all!* thought Fairatella. Freakadella also resented being mocked and ridiculed by others, and secretly wished that she could dress up in pretty fairy dresses.

"Harmless enough; what's wrong with that?" Fairatella wondered and looked puzzled.

Attentively, she listened for more, but the whispers became faint and muddled once again; she came out of her trance and noticed the fairy lights disappearing.

*The moon wanes,* thought Fairatella, after looking up at the night sky. Dark clouds half covered the moon.

Distant whispers were scarcely audible. She was just about to turn away when she heard a faint whisper; she saw speckles of light on the lake's surface again, and the moon shone dimly as the clouds passed by.

On hearing her name, her ears pricked up, and she listened for one last time; a soft echo in her ear said, "Fairatella, Chosen One..."

Concentrating hard, she gathered her wits again and waited.

"She who is pure of heart may release the curse..." Then the whispers faded forever.

Total silence unnerved her, and she spoke out loud for the first time since the whispers had begun.

"Lost moon, I hoped to learn more," Fairatella said disappointedly, whilst looking up at the dark side of the moon. Feeling drained, she fell to her knees at the lakeside wearily and then she sat and cuddled up into a ball, her tail wrapped around her as if to comfort her.

Mr. Mumble Bee and Pan had been watching Fairatella silently throughout the whole witching hour; to them, it seemed like Fairatella was telling one of her tale's in mime. By the way she had acted, they weren't very optimistic that she'd discovered anything of value. Suddenly, Eleganza landed beside Fairatella, taking her by surprise.

"You're back!" Fairatella exclaimed.

Eleganza hastened to reassure her that she was fine and said, "If needs be, I can fly with only one pair of wings."

Delighted to see Eleganza was well enough to fly again, Fairatella was eager to confide all that had taken place at the lake and all that she had heard as best as she could and expressed how mind boggling it had been for her. Also, that she feared she hadn't learned anything of great importance which could help her when confronted by Freakadella face to face.

Fairatella frowned and said, "I can't see how her being my aunt is going to save my buttocks!" Then she scratched her head and said, "I'm so muddled and I'm not really sure whether I've found out anything or not!"

On seeing that Fairatella was disheartened, Eleganza very wisely said, "What makes no sense now, at the right time will become crystal clear." Her words encouraged Fairatella and helped her to see things from a different perspective.

Fairatella smiled and said, "Very true, Eleganza, thank you for pointing that out to me."

Eleganza encouraged her further and said, "Besides, you must be feeling exhausted by now; you need to rest. I'm sure you'll see everything differently after a good night's sleep."

Fairatella agreed and remembered that Serena had suggested that if in need, she could take refuge on the tiny fairy isle in the middle of the lake.

Eleganza had been there before and said, "It's the perfect place to rest. No harm shall come to us there."

"All aboard for Fairy Isle!" shouted Eleganza, which woke Mr. Mumble Bee from his snooze; he tried to look alert and on standby. Pan was reluctant to leave, the idea of flying again made him feel nauseous and he much rather preferred to stay by the lakeside. Fairatella reassured him it was only a short distance away.

Fairatella, Eleganza, Mr. Mumble Bee and Pan all set off for the Fairy Isle. Although it was an easy flight for Eleganza with no obstacles in the way, she still proceeded with care, as they were near to Freakadella's domain. Eleganza was well aware that Freakadella's messengers might be on night patrol, scouting nearby territory. No one spoke. Eleganza flew smoothly and slowly so Mr. Mumble Bee could fly by her side; she didn't want to lose him, and she also didn't want to strain herself, as her wing still needed time to heal. It wasn't long before Fairatella set eyes on the Isle's shielding mist; it really did look like a dragon with outstretched wings. A wind had picked up and the dragon mist actually looked like it was flapping its wings. They passed through the mist, flew over the shore and then gradually gained height. It was dark, and the moon and stars shone faintly on the Isle, but Fairatella could tell that Eleganza knew exactly where she was going; she was a confident pilot and steered well despite flying downwind. After a short while, Eleganza landed in what Fairatella thought was the hollow of an old, tall tree.

"Make yourselves comfortable everyone, this is our shelter for tonight; it's warm and it will protect us from the blowing wind," said Eleganza, short of breath.

Fairatella could barely see, so she lit a tiny tea light she found and looked around her. On seeing a comfy bed of leaves, ashes from a burnt-out fire and scraps of food, she thought, *Someone has been here before.* Eleganza saw her concern and reassured her it was a safe place to rest, as only good folk and friends of Serena knew of its whereabouts.

Pan was already fast asleep. Mr. Mumble Bee looked at him, all droopy-eyed, and yawned before he slumped to the floor, snoring. Even Eleganza was exhausted and was resting in a comfy corner of the hollow with her wings out like a glider. Fairatella's eyes felt heavy, as she stared at the smouldering wick of the tea light. So physically and mentally exerted was Fairatella that as soon as she laid her weary head down on the comfy, dry leaves, she went out like a light.

# CHAPTER FOURTEEN

*Dark Hollows: Part One*
*En Route to the Old Stone Bridge*

The early bird woke Fairatella; she was still feeling drowsy, but she made an effort to get up after remembering Serena had advised her to get an early start. Mr. Mumble Bee was already awake and feeling cranky because he'd not slept well due to Fairatella flipping about in her sleep. She was flippant with him and said, "What did you expect, sleepy head? Did you presume that I'd sleep well after what happened yesterday? 'Did it even occur to you that I might be anxious about today?'

"Buzzy, buzzy, buzzy," said Mr. Mumble Bee, before he buzzed off quickly, pretending to be busy, as he had seen how agitated she was.

As she looked out of the hollow, sleepy-eyed and stretched her arms, she was surprised to see the most spectacular view, so she rubbed her eyes quickly to make sure that she wasn't dreaming, as she thought she was looking down onto the Garden of Eden. They were on top of the Isle. Her senses came to and she realised that it must have rained lightly during the night, as she could smell wet grass and a sweet fragrance of wild flowers in the air. The morning dew glistened on the tree leaves around her. Wide awake, she couldn't believe her eyes; she'd not taken refuge in a hollow after all, and she was way up high on a treetop, in a fairy tree house, a cosy little home decorated with dried flowers. Ivy curtains hung like garlands over the windows and wind chimes hung from the doorway, that when blown by the breeze made flute sounds. She looked up and saw an intricate dream catcher hanging from the log ceiling, and an acorn lampshade also caught her eye.

"What a charming little tree house. Daisy would love to play up here, it's the perfect lookout post too," said Fairatella, looking down below.

"Gosh, it's so high up, we're on top of the world, it's breath-taking! It must have been constructed by fairies; it's flawless," said Fairatella, as she marvelled at the handy craftsmanship. "Surely only winged creatures could possibly live up here." She felt a bit dizzy, and if it hadn't been for her tail she would have lost her balance.

Then Fairatella looked out to see beyond the Isle, but the thick mist that still shielded it from the outside world blinded her. Within her little world it was a bright summer's morn. *It would be so much easier if we could just stay here,* she thought whilst admiring the view, and sighed. The whispers she'd heard at the lake echoed in her ears and she recalled her task at hand, which made her stomach turn. A hunger pang brought her back to the present moment, and even though she didn't really feel like eating anything, she knew she had to gain strength for defeating Freakadella. She spotted appetising fruit in the orchards below; apricots and plums caught her fancy and she bent over the edge slightly, then took a deep breath. Fairatella, impulsive, daringly seized the moment by sky-diving off the tree house.

"Whoa!" she shouted, as she took the plunge, blown about like a feather.

The enthralling sensation stirred her adrenaline and made her senses hyper; in that moment, she felt more alive than ever before. With outspread wings, she swooped. Her upright tail looked like a propeller. Just before she reached the ground, she flapped her wings vigorously and started an upward climb, then downwards and eased off before landing.

"Thrilling," she exclaimed.

Thirstily, she drank fresh dewdrops, then shook a few leaves for more and said, "A real treat!" After she quenched her thirst she darted off to gather fruit.

Fairatella ate what she had freshly picked for breakfast. Eleganza, being carnivorous, caught a mosquito or two; Mr. Mumble Bee got lost in a plot of goldenrod, overwhelmed by the amount of pollen and nectar he could consume, and Pan, happy to be free again, drank water from the nearby spring. Fairatella filled up Pan's jar with cool spring water and threw in some leaves with algae on them that she'd collected from the stream before putting him back inside. He looked miserable, so she treated him to a mealworm.

After they'd all replenished themselves, it was time for them to continue their quest. Pan, out of the blue, refused to go with them. He begged Fairatella to leave him at the spring.

Pan cried out, "Flying doesn't agree with me, swimming does, I have no wings, see!" and then wriggled about a bit.

Almost relieved about not having to carry him any more, Fairatella decided it was for the best to leave him there, since the spring seemed like a safe enough place for him to stay.

*After all, the spring only flows into the lake, what possible harm could come to him here?* she pondered, whilst making sure he had ample algae leaves to eat and hide under nearby; she even found him a few bloodworms. Next, she placed his jar horizontally so that it only filled halfway up with water and secured it between some small rocks.

"There, precious Pan, now you can come and go as you please," said Fairatella fondly.

Pan was pleased as punch and bade her goodbye and, as an afterthought, said, "May the sacred elements guide you, and remember you're invincible when you want to be." He gave her his biggest tadpole smile.

She appreciated his encouragement and smiled back at him, although she was already missing him.

Eleganza regretted having to interrupt them and said apologetically, "Sorry but we must make haste."

Fairatella quickly hopped on to Eleganza's back and waved at Pan. Mr. Mumble Bee did the same since he was feeling as stuffed as a honey bear.

Pan had a sudden impulse to shout, "Till later!"

"Till then!" shouted back Fairatella, knowing full well that she might never return, but at least he could still survive in the spring if she didn't.

Airborne once again, this time they were bound for Dark Hollows. They flew up and over the Isle, then down on to the other side. When they passed through the shielding mist, Fairatella looked for the trail that led to the Black River. Eleganza had already seen it and was losing height fast; she told Mr. Mumble Bee it was about time he started to use his own wings and to follow her. Shortly after, they were flying over the trail and Fairatella noticed that it was just a mud track, but a dangerous one if taken on foot. She could see the Black River in the near distance; fortunately, the river was still black.

*Thank goodness! If Freakadella had taken any recent victims, the water flowing would be blood red,* thought Fairatella, as she remembered that Serena had warned her about the colour.

Eleganza flew low over the river, so low she actually glided over some parts of it, enabling Fairatella to sink her feet into the cool water. She felt like she was jet skiing. Mr. Mumble Bee, however, didn't appreciate getting drenched by Fairatella's foot splashing, and he was already struggling to keep up with them as usual. He managed to dodge some splashing, but he had to zigzag most of the way. Fairatella wondered if Eleganza was flying so low to avoid being seen.

*I suppose we do look rather conspicuous, a fairy riding on the back of a dragonfly and being followed by a bizarre bee,* thought Fairatella.

Taking great precautions so as not to be seen as they approached the stepping stones, Eleganza kept close to the riverbank. She was quick and agile when swerving over its bumpy contours; she could change direction in an instant.

Catching sight of the stepping stones from afar, Fairatella thought they looked like the humps of a dragon's backbone sticking out of the water. She half expected a dragon to suddenly emerge, which made her uneasy. Fairatella could see that the first stepping stone was stained with dried blood. The smell of burnt wood was pungent in the air, and she wondered if the stones were actually burnt tree stumps.

*The trees must have been hit by lightning, or someone must have burnt them down on purpose,* she thought, and then suddenly remembered that she had to cross the rushing river alone. She informed Eleganza, but she was already aware of the situation.

"Less conspicuous that way," said Eleganza.

"I suppose, but Serena also said the stepping stones must be crossed one by one for safety reasons, due to Freakadella's invisible force field hanging above them!" said Fairatella, on the ball.

Eleganza never even batted an eyelash. So Fairatella continued talking strategy.

Fairatella updated her further: "She also said that from now on, it's easy to be intercepted by Freakadella's messengers."

At first Fairatella hoped to catch Eleganza's interest, but instead she grasped that Eleganza probably knew more than she did, and it also occurred to her that Eleganza was withholding any gory details so as not to frighten her. Serena had never told Fairatella that there was a risk of being intercepted by Batty and Battier's bat radar or being seen from afar by Scarecrow, Scab and Scar's keen eye, nor about the electrifying force field above the stones that could sizzle you. Eleganza was well aware of all the risks.

"It would be so much easier just to fly across the stones or stumps, or whatever they are," said Fairatella, bearing in mind that the stones were bewitched and that she could only step on each stone once, or else she'd be bound to them and at the mercy of Freakadella forever.

Freakadella saw to it that no one crossed the river, neither airborne nor by the stepping stones.

"You first. I'll be right behind you," said Eleganza.

Fairatella nodded but never uttered a word. She took a deep breath and composed herself then she leaped for the first stone. Like an acrobat, she landed perfectly on one foot, whilst stretching out her other leg with her arms open wide to keep her balance. Her left foot then raised up onto tiptoe and she used her tail to help push her forward by making a whiplash movement and leapt again and landed effortlessly onto her right foot. She performed more daring acrobatics as she crossed the stepping stones carefully one by one. Before long, she had reached the last stone and was about to jump to shore when she looked back over her shoulder only to see that Mr. Mumble Bee had vanished, as she was used to him doing, but so had

Eleganza. Troubled, she scanned the riverbank, but they were nowhere to be seen.

As she turned back around to leap for shore, she slipped and lost her balance and almost fell into the water but saved herself instead by making a spectacular somersault before landing upside down on one hand. Her upright tail helped her to find her balance; she looked down at her hand and was shocked to see that it was all bloody, and then she realised she must have slipped on the very same blood. Horrified, she acted on impulse and did a one-handed handspring off the last stone, on to the riverbank opposite, and quickly regained her balance. Filled with disgust, she knelt by the riverside to wash her bloody hand, but to her dismay blood was flowing in the river, too. She looked to the left and right of the river and saw that blood was only flowing in some parts; it almost looked like blood rushing through veins, and so she quickly washed her hand in clear water whilst she still could.

Looking across to the other side of the river, she still saw no signs of Eleganza or Mr. Mumble Bee. Unsure what she should do next, she tried to remain calm and listen to her inner voice, but that proved to be too difficult since she was overcome with worry. She listened to reason and decided to continue alone.

"I've come this far and I'm not turning back now. I'm not giving up hope! They'll catch me up soon enough. Now all I have to do is follow the riverbank till I reach the old stone bridge," Fairatella said to herself.

She took one last glance at the blood-stained steppingstones and then proceeded along the riverbank. As she walked along cautiously, she noticed the landscape around her changing and thought, *The looming trees really do shroud the landscape in darkness; Serena was right.* A twig snapped, and that made her jump, and Fairatella whispered, "It must be really spooky here at night, I can just see the will-o'-the wisp drawing me from my safe path." She shuddered a little but continued ahead nevertheless. The further down the river she went, the darker the trees became; they haunted her, so she was constantly looking behind her to see if she'd been followed, but it was only tree shadows looming over her, playing tricks on her mind.

All by herself, she followed the lonely riverbank, keeping her eyes peeled, alert for any kind of foe. She wished that Eleganza was with her, and she even missed Mr. Mumble Bee and wondered what could have happened to them and hoped that they were safe.

During their disappearance, however, Eleganza and Mr. Mumble Bee had been very preoccupied with Freakadella's three messengers. They had backtracked to divert Scarecrow, Scab and Scar, the scavenger crows, from following Fairatella. Eleganza had spotted them out of the corner of her eye, flying overhead whilst she was watching Fairatella cross the river. Alarmed, thinking they might see Fairatella, Eleganza told Mr. Mumble Bee that they had to make a diversion quickly.

"Follow me, do as I do," said Eleganza urgently, and she started on an upward flight, then spun around in circles as fast as she could. Mr. Mumble Bee copied her; he stretched out his wings to keep up with her and in doing so they created a small whirlwind. She hummed, and Mr. Mumble Bee buzzed, both as loud as they could. It was enough to draw the crow's attention, and when they first caught sight of the whirlwind from afar, they became curious and started to fly towards it. Upon closer inspection, they saw that the whirlwind was actually a dragonfly and bumblebee chasing one another, and peered at them inquisitively, as they thought they were in a squabble of some kind, but they still nose-dived to intercept them. As Scarecrow, Scab and Scar approached, they looked very intimidating, and Eleganza realised that they should go in different directions, so she gave orders to Mr. Mumble Bee.

"You go east, and I'll go west, as far away as possible from Fairatella. Meet me at the old stone bridge after you've lost them," commanded Eleganza, and Mr.

Mumble Bee nodded obediently. Off they flew in different directions, to confuse the crows.

Mr. Mumble Bee shouted, "Over here, you cranky old crows," to coerce them into following him.

Eleganza waved her wing at them and then beckoned them to follow her before she started darting from place to place, high and low.

The crows were quick to catch on. Scarecrow, the leader and the sharpest, signalled for Scar to follow Mr. Mumble Bee and for Scab to stay with him to hunt down Eleganza, as she was the faster of their two preys.

Scar was far swifter than Mr. Mumble Bee, with him being so short and stubby, and he caught up to him in no time. Nevertheless, Mr. Mumble Bee haphazardly flapped his wings until Fairatella was far out of sight and then came to a sudden stop. With a wallop from Scar's wing he overturned Mr. Mumble Bee, causing him to lose his balance momentarily. When he was only a few inches away from him, face to face, Scar scowled at Mr. Mumble Bee and then opened up his beak to threaten him, but Mr. Mumble Bee just made fun of him by blowing raspberries.

"Crackpot crow, you don't scare me, Scar," said Mr. Mumble Bee as he goggled his eyes at him and stuck out his tongue, impersonating a nitwit.

Angered immensely by Mr. Mumble Bee's antics, Scar got ready to attack and cawed at him, but Mr. Mumble Bee never even flinched.

Instead, Mr. Mumble Bee just said, "Poof," then vanished into thin air, taking Scar by surprise.

Scar was furious and flew off in a temper to find Scarecrow and Scab, knowing full well he'd be scorned by Scarecrow for losing Mr. Mumble Bee even though he was now invisible. Mr. Mumble Bee was careful to stay out of sight until Scar was far away, then he cautiously made his way to the old stone bridge.

In the meantime, Eleganza was being chased by Scarecrow and Scab. Her ability to zip and zoom made her no easy catch. When she had led them far away from Fairatella, she stopped dead, causing them to bang into one another, which amused her greatly, but annoyed them.

Scarecrow feasted his eyes on Eleganza before she started to fly backwards away from him, and he said ironically, "Supper is served, Scab!"

Scab sniggered.

Whilst hovering in one spot, Eleganza quickly looked around for her next escape route, but the crows were getting too close, so she went from a dead halt to about 90 mph in just a few seconds to escape. At that point, she saw the river below her and dive-bombed straight for it. Just before she hit the water, she made a right-angled turn and changed direction in an instant, and then skimmed the water's surface so gracefully even the crows were impressed. They followed her but collided clumsily and belly flopped into the water. Seizing her opportunity to escape, she flew faster than ever before, despite her wounded wing. She followed the riverbank upstream and only slowed down when she'd lost the crows, then she dropped with exhaustion, forcing herself to rest for a while. As soon as she had recovered, she set off for the old stone bridge and hoped she would be able to catch up with Fairatella soon.

# CHAPTER FIFTEEN

### Dark Hollows: Part Two
### Freakadella's Lair

A storm was brewing by the time Fairatella reached the bloody bog. She shivered at the thought of what lay in the bog. *The bloody sight alone is enough to give anyone the creeps,* she thought. Not wanting to get bogged down with fears, she fixed her eyes on the old stone bridge opposite her. Determined not to get cold feet, she reasoned with herself: "I've come this far, it's not time for a weak will. Tivarnia is counting on me." Suddenly, a strong gust of wind lifted her off her feet. "Ha, the winds of change are blowing," she said, and flapped her wings and was one with the wind. Crossing the bog, her feet never touched the ground, and she landed on the foot of the bridge.

On standby, she looked all around her; fortunately, no one could be seen. She stood in silence for a moment and heard the wind howling. Serena's words came to mind. Once she'd crossed the bridge, there was no turning back. Taking her first step bravely, she became aware that the stone bridge bridged the gap between her and Freakadella, between good and evil. As she slowly crossed one step at a time, she also remembered that Freakadella could smell her presence.

*I also have a strong sense of smell, and something is surely cooking, and it reeks!* thought Fairatella, holding her nose as she went along. "Building a bridge of understanding between Freakadella and me seems highly unlikely... she's gonna eat me alive!" Then she repeated, "Have fairy faith," in her mind until she reached the end of the bridge.

Close at hand, she could see the wishing well; it looked like any other ordinary well, apart from the fact that crows were guarding it. She noticed the wooden sign hanging above the well, which had, 'Wishing You Well,' carved into it.

*I bet that's fooled one too many,* thought Fairatella. Then, a terrifying thought flashed through Fairatella's mind, that fierce, black crows had attacked some of Freakadella's victims while they were bending over the well to make a wish. Fairatella imagined that the well-wishers had heard a sudden, SQUAWK! before the black crows came swooping down, and hit them on the back of their heads. Cawing as they clawed at them and their talons drew blood, until the well-wishers lost their balance and tumbled into the well. They screamed whilst falling to their death. Fairatella remembered that a group of crows was called a murder. *Murder... A marauding murder of crows, are not to be trifled with,* thought Fairatella and she trembled.

Despite their perfect vision, the crows hadn't noticed Fairatella, as they were too busy quarrelling about their misfortunate hunt. Shocked and offended on seeing Fairatella only a few steps away from them, they stood to attention and looked hostile in defence of the well.

Scarecrow shouted, "No trespassing!"

Fairatella stood firmly and said loudly, "I'm not an intruder, I come in peace. I wish to speak with Freakadella."

Scarecrow, Scab and Scar all screeched with laughter, but their presence remained sinister.

Scarecrow replied, in a threatening tone, "Be careful what you wish for!"

He looked seriously at Fairatella and never took his eyes off her, whilst Scab and Scar convulsed with laughter, but she didn't find it the least bit funny.

Scarecrow gave them an order. "Shush, Scab and Scar, you idiots, can't you see that I'm trying to concentrate on my prey?"

They both looked at him sheepishly and said simultaneously, "Yes Scarecrow, oh wise one."

"Silence!" said Scarecrow, losing his temper, and then he scolded Scab and Scar for being compulsive talkers.

Scarecrow, in his frustration, was slow to realise that Fairatella was already aware of Freakadella's hideout, and when it finally clicked, it troubled him. *No one knows of Freakadella's whereabouts... how could she have possibly found out?* thought Scarecrow, unsure of what he was supposed to do or say next; he simply scowled at her.

Sharp-witted as Fairatella was, on hearing Scarecrow, Scab and Scar's names, the strange whisper she'd heard at the lake that she could make no sense of suddenly became very clear to her, and she thought, *Ha, luck favours the brave, it's the flipping password!*

Scarecrow

Scab

Scar

She concentrated for a moment longer. "It was repeated, so..." Fairatella quickly blurted out their names once. "Scarecrowscabandscar."

Scarecrow didn't know what hit him; before he had the chance to do anything Fairatella repeated their names another two times, revealing the secret password for entering the well. The crows fell automatically into a trancelike state, docile as lambs, and they said together, "Permission to enter is granted," whilst staring into space.

Not knowing how long the trance would last for, Fairatella acted with promptness and quickly lowered the water bucket down into the well, as far as it would go. Using the rope seemed like the easiest way to go down. Climbing down the well monkey-like, she used her tail to guide her way through the dark and coiled it around the rope to secure herself when she got unsteady. The descent down the well was difficult, because it was so deep, and the further down she went, the darker it got. She hurried down, hoping to see a light soon from below.

The flapping of wings beneath Fairatella startled her and she froze. Then something slippery brushed past her arm. On realising it was a bat, she became squeamish, as she loathed them, and could hardly contain herself.

"Detestable creatures," Fairatella exclaimed; the idea of them alone could make her flesh creep. All at once, a swarm of bats swept by her and frightened her to death. Panic-stricken, she thought, *Blind as a bat, they say, so they can't see me; they use radar to sense their way, but they seem to be on the move, so it's not me they're after. Calm, just keep calm!*

Then one bat got caught up in her hair; disgusted by it, she screamed and flung her arms up in the air, letting go of the rope. Shaking her head and flipping her hair, she desperately tried to untangle it as she fell deeper down the well. Eventually, she managed to release it, after being tossed about hither and thither. She was being sucked up like a fly into a vacuum cleaner.

"This well is never-ending," she said, scared.

As she gained velocity, she lost control and was overcome with fear. Fairatella recalled her premonition about falling down a dark well, feeling like a fragile dandelion being blown in the wind, and thought, *But I saw a strange cavern, too, I remember I sensed an evil presence there; it must lead to a cavern sooner or later.*

Suddenly she banged her head; she'd hit the bottom of the well with great impact and remembered nothing from that moment on. She lay there, unconscious, and was barely breathing.

Down came Eleganza and Mr. Mumble Bee, charging to her rescue, but after seeing her stillness, they feared they were too late. Fairatella gave her last breath just as they arrived. Heartbroken, Eleganza and Mr. Mumble Bee looked upon her in silence, their eyes swelled with tears.

Eleganza said, with great remorse, "We have failed you, Chosen One."

When all seemed lost, Fairatella's pouch started to glow; the wishing star shone bright and then a healing light covered Fairatella from head to toe. All aglow, she levitated. Eleganza and Mr. Mumble Bee saw the life rush back into her miraculously, and they jumped for joy, wreathed in smiles. At first, Fairatella couldn't even recall her own name, but when she saw Eleganza and Mr. Mumble Bee beside her, moved to tears, all that had happened flashed before her eyes.

Fully awake, and with a look of astonishment, Fairatella said, "I'm not dead after all. Luck be a cat today, I've got nine lives, well, still eight to go!"

It wasn't only her tail that made her different from other fairies; she had cat's luck too.

Fairatella threw back her head and popped a seed and said, "Better make that two," I've just lost a life today!" She chuckled. Knowing that she had eight more lives to live gave her courage and she felt invincible.

Little did she know that as she felt invincible one minute, when faced with evil, she would soon feel so easily defeated the next.

Flames of fire drew her attention and lit up the mouth of the cavern by chance. It was Puffin practicing his fire throwing, but they didn't know that then. Puffin disappeared, and they found themselves in darkness again.

"Not to worry, the wishing star can lead the way in the dark," said Fairatella.

Holding the star in the palm of her hand, she guided them, and they proceeded into the cavern. Stalactites and stalagmites had sprouted like teeth; she imagined that she was entering into the mouth of a dragon. That sickly smell soon brought her back to reality; the one she had first smelt whilst crossing the bridge now filled the underground cavern strongly. It was such a disagreeable smell even Eleganza and Mr. Mumble Bee had to hold their noses. Fairatella, however, had gotten used to it. She wondered if that was the reason why Freakadella hadn't been able to smell her presence yet.

*What's cooking?* thought Fairatella, *Smells like a concoction of smoked rotten meat and vomit. What's that mean witch up to this time?* She started to feel nauseous and claustrophobic.

Fairatella whispered to her loyal following, "I definitely don't have a partiality for cave dwelling. How does that old troglodyte live here, day in, day out, surrounded by darkness?"

She couldn't even imagine how Freakadella could feel at home living underground, never seeing the light of day; she assumed that her soul must be shadowed by darkness too. Bravely, Fairatella led the way deeper into the bottomless cavern. Eleganza and Mr. Mumble Bee tagged along right behind her, since they were afraid of the dark. She followed her nose until the stench got so overpowering she was sure she was getting close to Freakadella's abode. Smoke billowed in front of her; she stepped into a cloud of smoke and covered her mouth to prevent herself from coughing.

"This must be the Smoke Chamber," said Fairatella, trying to humour the others, but she proceeded with caution nevertheless, as she was well aware there was no smoke without fire. Passing through the smoke-filled chamber wasn't easy, and they gasped for air. Fairatella heard the sound of water dripping nearby. Drops of water trickled down the stalactites; she caught a few drops in her hand and sprinkled them onto her face gladly, then again to wash her smoky eyes.

One chamber led to another; the one ahead was now ablaze, and flames licked the smoke-blackened walls. As she approached closer, she noticed that the flames stopped and started again, which made her curious as to the cause of the fire. Then, before her very eyes, she saw a smoke-covered dragon and from what she could gather, it seemed to be practicing its flame throwing. It was Puffin, Freakadella's pet. Fairatella thought it odd since she'd never seen a dragon before, and she presumed that it was a baby due to its size but compared to her it was still large. It was dark, so she could only really see him when he was lit up by a fiery background; she noticed his jagged silhouette and marvelled at it.

All at once, muttering could be heard from the distance. Fairatella stopped dead in her tracks, which caused Eleganza and Mr. Mumble Bee to bump into the back of her.

"Shhh, I thought I heard something," Fairatella whispered.

Then, without prior warning, Freakadella shrieked, "Puffin! Stop that now, you pathetic excuse of a dragon! I can't concentrate!"

Her angry voice echoed throughout the cavern, a glass-shattering sound that really shook them up. Panicky, Mr. Mumble Bee looked at Fairatella all goggle-eyed and gulped; unnerved, Eleganza just kept looking from left to right, half expecting Freakadella to pounce on them at any moment. Afterwards, they all saw Puffin running for cover with his tail between his legs as sparks flew in the air. He hid from Freakadella to avoid her sparks and scorn. The whites of Puffin's eyes stood out in the dark, making it easy for Fairatella to spot him from a distance. She noticed that Puffin had his huge eyes wide-open, and that they moved to-and-fro, from side to side in fear.

"Even the dragon is afraid of her, albeit a baby one," whispered Fairatella, whilst thinking of her next move. She knelt to the ground and signalled with her hand for Eleganza and Mr. Mumble Bee to lie low and to follow her. Crawling from one rock to another, Fairatella, tagged closely by Eleganza and Mr. Mumble Bee, zigzagged their way on the ground, until Freakadella was in sight.

# CHAPTER SIXTEEN

## *Eye to Eye*

A fire was burning, and a cauldron was bubbling. Freakadella was busy making a new misfit broth. She couldn't be seen properly as she was bent over the cauldron and stirring the broth attentively. The stench of it had indeed prevented Freakadella from smelling Fairatella's presence, and anything else, come to that. Unexpectedly, Freakadella got wind of her; she stopped what she was doing immediately, her nostrils flared, and she inhaled a whiff of her likely victim and looked about her warily.

"Who goes there? Who dares to enter my home uninvited? Reveal yourself!" shouted Freakadella at the top of her voice, terrifying everyone in sight.

Thousands of bats suddenly scattered everywhere, fleeing as far out of sight as possible. Fairatella froze for a second, and then gathered her wits after remembering to always have fairy faith and to trust her fairy instinct. She boldly came out from behind the rock to reveal herself, and so did Eleganza and Mr. Mumble Bee, reluctantly.

They all stared at Freakadella with their mouths wide open. Freakadella's eyes gleamed as she feasted on her prey. She had a special craving for fairy flesh; she twiddled her plebian thumbs, and then licked them. Freakadella's eyesight was fading due to living in darkness, so she beckoned them closer with her claw-like finger to gloat better.

"Aha, come closer and introduce yourselves, it's not polite to stare," said Freakadella fervently.

As Fairatella approached, her teeth started to chatter, as the sight of Freakadella was blood curdling. She thought, *She really is too ugly to be seen, even in the dark.*

Fairatella started to feel queasy, too, and then it dawned on her that the cauldron must be made of iron; fairies hate iron and won't go near it, as it gives them headaches and makes them feel terribly nauseous.

Despite her feeling sickly and scared, she still found the courage to introduce herself to Freakadella. "I'm Fairatella," she said, and turned around to introduce the others, "and this is Eleganza and Mr. Mumble Bee."

But Freakadella shooed them away and dismissed them with a wave of her hand; it was Fairatella she was interested in.

"Stay, skinny one! Why are you here?" said Freakadella, demanding an answer.

"I've come all the way from Milky Brooks to request that you release the spell you put on me and all the other misfits of Tivarnia," said Fairatella; her voice quivered, and her knees shook as she spoke.

Intrigued, but also suspicious, Freakadella said, "That's the flimsiest excuse I've ever heard." Then she chuckled sinisterly which made them all squirm.

After that her tone changed to one of anger, and she shouted, "Why should I, the almighty Freakadella, help the likes of you? A miserable looking fairy at that!"

She reached out her hand and grabbed Fairatella by the hair and pulled at it hard, pulling her closer to take a better look at her. Pulling her head backwards with the one hand, and with the other grabbing hold of her jaw, she squeezed hard. She breathed on Fairatella, and her breath was awful; it stank so much that Fairatella had to turn her head away. Just as Freakadella lowered her hand and spread her fingers wide, about to grab Fairatella by the throat, Mr. Mumble Bee charged to the rescue and stung Freakadella right in her thick-skinned neck. He did so knowing full well it would be the death of him, as honeybees can sting only once. His stinger was torn off as it lodged into her skin. Freakadella let go of Fairatella's hair abruptly so she could grab hold of Mr. Mumble Bee; she wanted to crush him with her bare hands, but she wasn't fast enough and lost sight of him. By the time Fairatella recovered, Mr. Mumble Bee was already on the ground, lying on his back with his legs in the air after having had a massive abdominal rupture. Fairatella watched the life drain out of him within minutes. Horrified that Mr. Mumble Bee had given his life for hers in her hour of need, she couldn't hold back her tears.

Fearing Freakadella would harm Eleganza, too, Fairatella frantically turned around to warn her, but Eleganza had already fled from the cavern. Relieved that Eleganza was safe, she turned back and looked Freakadella straight in the eye. Something snapped inside of her.

Overcome with anger, Fairatella cried out, "No!" She tried to release herself from Freakadella's grip by punching and kicking her. She fought tooth and nail but Freakadella was far stronger than her, and she seized Fairatella by the neck with both hands. Although she was being choked, she still didn't give up and croaked, "Ugly witch..."

As soon as Freakadella set eyes on the double heart-shaped locket, she stopped choking her and loosened her grip. Her manic expression turned to one of surprise, then to one of regret most unexpectedly, but only momentarily. "Where did you get that locket from, thief?" asked Freakadella. She still had hold of Fairatella by the throat and she squeezed, just hard enough so that she was still able to talk.

"Mother," stammered Fairatella. "Bellarosea." Fairatella remembered the whisper at the lake, revealing that her mother was Freakadella's sister. *Why didn't I mention it before?* she thought, cross with herself for being tongue-tied when finally face to face with Freakadella, and that her plan of action had turned to smoke.

Freakadella believed that Bellarosea was her mother, but only after examining her closely; she'd been so blinded by anger that she never even noticed her cat's tail, her big, bright cat eye's and her unusually small wings. She let go of Fairatella when it dawned on her that she really was telling the truth, not because she felt merciful, but because she had a compelling curiosity. She wanted to learn more about her niece and what else she had to *say. Does she know she's my niece?* wondered Freakadella, *and how did she learn of my secret whereabouts?* Freakadella was very curious to find out, but she was also annoyed for not realising sooner that she was Bellarosea's precious daughter and damned her failing eyesight.

Fully aware that she had not yet escaped the wrath of Freakadella, as she sensed that she was very crafty, Fairatella decided that her next plan of action would be to play along with her aunt. *You've not met with the likes of me before, you mean witch; never underestimate a fairy,* she thought, as she took a glance at poor Mr. Mumble Bee and summoned up the courage to confront Freakadella once and for all.

"I know you are my aunt," said Fairatella firmly, and looked Freakadella straight in the eye.

"Aunt, eh?" sniggered Freakadella, "and who told you that?" She tried not to show that she was a bit piqued.

Fairatella noticed a change in her voice, but she couldn't quite put her finger on it, so she continued, "I heard it whispered at the lake."

Freakadella was all ears now. "Aha, and who, pray, told you about the Lake of All Whispering Secrets?" Fairatella's silence made her impatient and she glared at her with piercing eyes. "You're not chickening out now, are you, chicken wings?" said Freakadella, provoking her. While she waited for an answer, she admired her handiwork; her dissimilarity amused her greatly.

In her silence, Fairatella was buying time so she could concentrate on all the other secrets whispered regarding Freakadella. After she recalled them, she looked at her wings, then at Freakadella, and said calmly, "I stumbled upon the lake when in need of rest; as you can see my little wings can't carry me that far."

The inquisition wasn't over yet, and she leered at Fairatella. Freakadella's suspicious nature always got the best of her, and whilst rapt in thought she frowned and squinted at Fairatella till she concluded that someone must have told Fairatella of her whereabouts. Furthermore, someone had encouraged her, as it was quite out of character for a tiny fairy to be so daring. *Either I have a messenger traitor in the midst, or someone else with magical powers can escape my evil eye. There is only one possible being capable of that in the whole of Tivarnia. That crafty Serena is behind all of this; wait till I get my hands on that goody two shoes, she'll be sorry for meddling in my affairs,* thought Freakadella. Her blood started to boil; she gave

Fairatella a deadly look and said in an entreating tone, "Who told you that I put that spell on you? Serena?"

Although Fairatella was in a tight spot, she was still able to focus and replied, "Oh, that's easy, all of Tivarnia knows that you're notorious as the misfit witch." Then she paused for a while and then said, "Serena? Who's she? Never heard of her."

Smiling with satisfaction, Freakadella felt flattered; her ego was boosted, and it showed, so much so she almost forgot about Serena.

On noticing her few crooked teeth and cracked lips, Fairatella thought, *I've never seen such a dreadful and fearsome smile before, she is extremely ugly!* She almost felt sorry for her, as she recalled how Freakadella had wished to be prettier than Bellarosea. *That would have taken a huge makeover, I bet,* she thought, whilst observing Freakadella's freakiness. *That's it, she needs a makeover, why didn't I think of that before!* Ecstatic about her new brainwave, Fairatella set about convincing her how much prettier she would look with a little make-up, a new hairstyle and perhaps some new clothes.

At first, Freakadella thought that she was mocking her and didn't take her seriously, but something about Fairatella's voice made her believe that she was sincere. Freakadella wasn't capable of trusting anyone, but she thought she should at least try out the idea and see what came of it. Perhaps she reminded her of her sister Bellarosea, as childhood memories came flooding back that she thought she had forgotten about for good, and gradually she softened to the makeover idea. "Show me," said Freakadella in a commanding tone, still wary of her. She didn't let down her guard, especially as she was aware that fairies could create illusions.

Fairatella thought hard until she could visualise Freakadella with a new improved look; it had to be believable or else her powers of persuasion would fail. Taking longer than expected, Freakadella became impatient and she never took her eyes off Fairatella whilst she was creating a new look. As she watched her nod and shake her head, knit her fingers together when she approved of an idea and wave away her hands when rejecting an idea, Freakadella did exactly the same. She copied her without even realising it, so engrossed by the whole performance. But she couldn't keep up with her, as she was constantly changing her mind.

"No, no, that won't do, that's awful, tut, tut, tut, appalling, umm that's better, and oh that might work, yes, yes, perfect!" said Fairatella, whilst working on her ideas.

When Fairatella had finally decided on a new look, Freakadella gave a sigh of relief; she was actually excited, and she couldn't wait to see the result and it was difficult for her to pretend otherwise. Next, Fairatella raised her hands slowly in the air, her feet lifted to tiptoe then off the ground, her wings outstretched but remained still and then she became all aglow as she levitated. After that, her floodlight eyes projected the illusion of the new look she had in mind, right in front of Freakadella for her to see, putting her in the spotlight, as if she was looking at her own reflection through a grand, gold flake mirror with dazzling potential.

Astonished by the results, Freakadella touched and caressed her face with her hand gently; her reflection did exactly the same. She took a few steps back and then swayed towards the mirror. She put one hand on her hip and flicked her hair back with the other. She flipped back her long black cape then whisked it aside, causing a gust of wind; Fairatella was jolted for a moment but quickly resumed her position and focused again. Fairatella detected that she couldn't walk very well in her high-heeled boots, and there was something about the way she moved that puzzled her, something quite not right, but she couldn't fathom it to fix it. She was eager to learn if Freakadella was pleased with the result. Up close, Freakadella could see herself much better as she had poor eyesight; she looked hard at herself for some time and then a tear came to her eye most unexpectedly. Fairatella took pity on her.

Suddenly, Freakadella became outraged and balled at Fairatella, "You wicked little fairy, making me see things that aren't really there!"

*Why the sudden change?* thought Fairatella, panic-stricken, *I thought I had her wrapped around my little finger.* Quickly trying to remember anything whispered about Freakadella, she charged fiercely towards her; she hoped a backup plan, would spring to mind. Backing away from her, she robustly stomped from side to side, and even the ground shook with terror. *What did I do to offend her? Everything seemed to be going so well. She looked a lot better, even feminine,* she thought, terrified, as she froze on the spot. A heavy punch came towards her; she unfroze and ducked just in time to miss the mighty blow. Whilst she was on the ground, she was surprised to see Freakadella's holy tights had huge thick hairs sticking out of them, and moreover how muscular her legs were. Suddenly it twigged. Freakadella wasn't her aunt after all; she was a he, and she shouted out spontaneously, "You're my uncle!" Stopping dead in his tracks, Freakadella was shocked and amazed that Fairatella had discovered the truth about him.

Her father's words rushed to mind, how he was so repulsed by Freakadella and her ways and, how when Freakadella was younger she wished to dress up in pretty fairy dresses. It all became so clear to her now. The tear that Freakadella had shed, after taking a closer look at himself in the mirror, was a tear of hopelessness, as he realised that a makeover couldn't make him into a real woman. He did look more agreeable, more feminine on the outside, but it still wasn't enough for him, as even though he felt like a woman on the inside, he was still trapped inside a man's body. He felt like he had been condemned to a life of male misery and longed for another life of female fantasy.

"Yes, I'm your uncle, the almighty Freakadella, the wicked witch who was once a flipping fairy! Laugh if you must," he confessed bitterly; he had his hands on his hips. He wondered if Fairatella would fear him less, now that his credibility had been damaged. Anticipating that she would ridicule him for not being an ordinary fairy, he stood awkwardly and looked the other way whilst waiting for her to respond.

She could sense his pain and solemnly said, "It is no laughing matter, laughter is for the happy." Fairatella gave him a smile of understanding. "I'm not one to judge, I'm no ordinary fairy either," she said sincerely. She took hold of her tail and gave it a swing and then looked over her shoulder at her small wings and said, "I know what it's like to be different." Her words struck a chord; they finally saw eye to eye on something. She listened to his grievances with an open mind. He felt he had been discriminated against because of his gender identity. Freakadella had lost hope of ever being understood long ago, and as Fairatella tried to penetrate through his layers of bitterness, he seemed to slowly crumble. With a sense of relief, he shared his pain. He revealed to Fairatella that his gender transition had been a struggle, and that he was devastated when he was looked upon as an outcast. For a moment, she saw his eyes light up, but it was only a fleeting flicker of hope. Her chance had slipped away. She knew it was too late, and there was nothing she could do; he had already perished in darkness. It was only a matter of time before he would be completely consumed by evil.

In total black despair, he reached out once again to grab her by the throat. Fairatella escaped his grasp by tripping him up with her tail. She was agile and a lot faster than he was, but as he fell, he snatched her locket and ripped it off from around her neck. He yelled at her, "You don't understand, you're not ugly like I am. I will not stop until Tivarnia becomes a cesspit of ugly misfits!" His curses showered down upon her and Tivarnia as he stumbled to his feet. He cursed her, saying, "Shrivel up like an old prune, food for cockroaches you'll become," and then he damned her soul.

In fear of failure, Fairatella had already reached desperately for the wishing star. "If there's an ounce of goodness left, the star will draw it out of him," she prayed. She decided to use her one and only wish, not to save herself but to warm Freakadella's bitter heart. Holding the wishing star tight in the palm of her hand, she then placed it close to her heart and said out loud, "Wishing star of olde, elders, grant me my wish. I wish for Freakadella to see the light in the dark."

Just in the nick of time, the wishing star activated an unknown source of energy, stopping time itself, and Freakadella froze on the spot. At first the star glowed, radiating heat, which warmed the cold cavern. Then rays of light illuminated the dark like a beacon of hope. The wishing star exploded into a thousand and one pieces and shook the cavern. A blinding light bathed Fairatella, and afterwards she shone like a bright star. She looked at her hands, which sparkled magically, and she approached Freakadella and laid her hands on his shoulders. With a healing touch, Freakadella awoke from darkness and became an enlightened spirit. Stupefied, Freakadella just gazed at Fairatella as she dazzled him; he'd never seen such a powerful light source before. Freakadella was still holding Fairatella's locket, so Fairatella reached out her hand indicating that she wanted him to give it back. He did so willingly and placed it in the palm of Fairatella's little hand.

Overjoyed, Fairatella kissed the locket, then shared her mother's secret with him. "My mother understood you. I heard her whisper at the lake that she felt sad because you couldn't find happiness. She even wished for you to be beautiful and popular. Before she died, she asked my father to give me this locket when I grew up, knowing that I would need it one day. I believe she forgave you for casting that spell on her; she must have loved you dearly."

Moved, Freakadella's eyes swelled with tears. "I gave it to her; it symbolises fraternity forever, our blood bond." He had a faraway look in his eyes as he reminisced about his childhood days; sweet memories with his sister Bellarosea warmed his heart. He broke down and sobbed, letting go of all his anger. After a short while, he composed himself and then hugged Fairatella unexpectedly. Whilst hugging her tightly, he said in a proud voice, "It took plenty of spunk to come here, you must take after me!" He squeezed her cheeks affectionately.

Fairatella laughed then said in all seriousness, "I came here because of Serena, but I stayed here because of you, Freakadella. There is good in everyone. No matter how deep in the soul it's hidden, you still have to look for it, even if it's covered with cobwebs you'll find it eventually. Goodness is like a gem that always burns bright."

A fragment of the wishing star sparkled on the ground and caught Fairatella's eye. She picked it up and looked at the inscription and said, "I wonder what it means?"

"It's ancient fairy, I think it says, 'The Chosen One'," said Freakadella; he had some knowledge of fairy antiquity.

"I believe it does," said Fairatella, and smiled when she thought that her task was nearly done. The wishing star had brought out the goodness in Freakadella. All she needed to do now was to persuade him to undo all his dark witchcraft and to make Tivarnia a land free of misfits again. But first, she remembered she still had Freakadella's makeover to do. When she looked upon him, Fairatella noticed that he already looked more attractive than he did before, now that he glowed with goodness. She set about giving Freakadella his new makeover, and Freakadella was ecstatic about the whole idea!

# CHAPTER SEVENTEEN

## *Drakess's Revenge*

All at once, the rumble of the cavern walls interrupted Freakadella from having his new hair styling done. Fairatella was jolted unexpectedly and ended up landing on her backside. The cavern shook from top to bottom. Then loud thudding and thumping noises could be heard coming towards them. Fairatella looked at Freakadella terrified, and she gulped as she thought that the cavern walls were going to cave in on them, but Freakadella didn't look the least bit afraid.

Fairatella shouted, "Whatever that is, it must be mammoth!"

At that instant, an enormous dragon flew swiftly towards them from afar, bringing light to the dark cavern with its fiery breath. Within moments a roaring fire was heading right for them, as the flaming dragon was burning everything in its path with a vengeance.

"Yikes, there's no escaping that fire!" shrieked Fairatella.

"It's Drakess the dragoness, her chains must have broken when the cavern shook earlier," Freakadella said loudly, and looked annoyed.

"Chains? What do you mean chains?" said Fairatella worriedly.

"I chained her when I took her baby Puffin for my pet," said Freakadella, admitting that he was responsible.

"You did what! That's all we need! You must have been deranged to do a thing like that!" Fairatella said, panic-stricken.

"Well Puffin is very cute," Freakadella said, looking a little ashamed after realising what he'd done.

"Great, now we have an unleashed dragoness on the rampage," shouted Fairatella. "An angry mother with a flaming temper at that. There's no wrath like a mother's scorn!" She backed away. "Any bright ideas, Freakadella, as you got us into this mess?" she said sarcastically.

"Apologise?" Freakadella said, as he raised his shoulders, and Fairatella squinted at him.

Before long Drakess was only a few steps away. She thumped her head against the cavern wall, then bawled, "Where is my baby Freakadella?" Their ears rang with her deafening tone. Drakess loomed over them, threatening their very existence. She was gigantic.

Fairatella looked up at her with her mouth wide open, then she gulped and said, "Looming doomsday is upon us!"

Seeking revenge, Drakess's eyes were fired with anger, her nostrils were flared and blazing, and she showed her teeth, huge white fangs gleaming amidst flaming red.

So distraught with fury was Drakess that she didn't seem to care about her own jagged tail being on fire. Like a whip she beat her tail to the ground, again and again, relentlessly. Her body was covered in thick, protective scales that were myriad shades of green.

Fairatella, being the great teller of tales that she was, was well aware that arrows just bounced off them and swords easily snapped when penetrating such scales, but she also knew that dragons had weak spots: the neck and stomach, where the scales were softer or even had no scales at all.

"But I have neither arrow nor sword, there must be another way... Dragons are immune to fairy magic too!" Various thoughts went through Fairatella's mind as she tried to summon up courage to do something. *But what?* she asked herself. She noticed that one of Drakess's feet still had a broken chain attached to it; the chain links had been smashed. Her coarse skin was cut from breaking free of the chains. Old scars were signs of her being captive before, and old wounds decorated her body like awarded medals earned for bravery. Drakess smelt like a burning pipe as she gave off smoke; smoky tobacco fumes reminded Fairatella of her father. She pictured him taking out his pipe and filling it with tobacco. Drakess stamped her foot down and brought her back to her terrifying reality. "Drakess is unbridled and rightly so, what mother wouldn't want to reclaim her baby? Just tell her where Puffin is," urged Fairatella. She wanted to assist Drakess and demanded that Freakadella tell her of his whereabouts.

"Where's Puffin?" bellowed Drakess, and she stooped down with a snakelike movement; her gigantic head was only inches away from them, and then she hissed, "He's not yours to keep!"

Scared to death, Fairatella blurted out, without taking a breath, "I saw him a while ago practicing flame throwing." Her fiery eyes looked right at Fairatella, intimidating her, and Fairatella took a deep breath and cried out, "In the upper chamber!" *Nothing short of a miracle can save us now,* thought Fairatella, losing hope for survival.

Having all the information she needed to know, Drakess had no use for them any more, and she was ready to burn them to cinders when Eleganza and Serena miraculously appeared out of nowhere.

Relieved to see them both, Fairatella realised that Eleganza had fled not out of fear but only to bring backup after seeing Mr. Mumble Bee valiantly fall to his death. Serena looked at Freakadella, and she could tell that he was no longer in darkness; Fairatella had succeeded and was the Chosen One after all, and now Serena had to protect her from the wrath of Drakess. Surprised to see Serena and Eleganza, Freakadella was glad to be aided at such a crucial moment, but he doubted that Serena possessed enough power to overcome Drakess's furious flames.

Raising her hand, Serena commanded Drakess, "Be gone!"

Drakess opened her large bat-like wings, and with a demonic expression she hissed, "Only after I have my revenge for what Freakadella has done. He must suffer the consequences and burn in Hell!"

Serena remained calm and replied mellifluously, almost mesmerising Drakess with her tone, "Freakadella has changed, he is sorry for what he has done," and turned towards Freakadella and urged him to agree. "Aren't you?" Freakadella nodded emphatically, but Drakess wasn't convinced.

"Do you mean that from the bottom of your heart?" said Drakess ironically, and then sniggered, "Witches don't have a heart!"

Freakadella replied truthfully, "I do, thanks to Fairatella the Chosen One. I was dying inside before she showed me that believing in something or someone is better than having an empty heart."

*Curiouser and curiouser,* thought Drakess, and repeated out aloud, "Chosen One?"

"She who brings peace to Tivarnia," said Freakadella, a believable convert.

Billows of smoke clouded the glimmer of hope for a peaceful outcome. Drakess was no longer able to contain her fury and she struggled to hold back her flames.

Eleganza realised that Drakess's behaviour was beyond reproach, so she spoke up after being silent and implored Drakess, "I was once a dragon, we are kin, so by dragon law that makes us allies. Let us settle this peacefully!"

"Allies," mocked Drakess, although she was well aware that creatures of the Fairy Realm often came in many shapes and sizes.

"Yes, my ancestors are your ancestors from three hundred million years ago. I was Drakena of Drianne, I burned everything in sight until there was nothing left to burn," said Eleganza, remorseful.

It was quite clear that Drakess had heard of her before as she raised her eyebrows in acknowledgement.

"I, Drakena, was caught by my very own magic and disguise, the art of illusion to change form. The greedy old wizard Greedion, with a promise of a new land to burn, tricked me into shape shifting into the form of a dragonfly, but really, he sought my precious hoard of treasure. Once I became a dragonfly, he saw to it that I couldn't shift back, and I've remained in that shape ever since, the dragonfly you see before you today. I am a victim of my own vanity; I lost my power by accepting his challenge to prove my magical prowess. Small and defenceless, my treasure was easily stolen from me, but later I found a greater treasure, one called compassion. The fairies showed me that and they also made me aware of my spiritual energy. Fairies are pure of heart and wish not to harm us, they only want for us all to live together in harmony. I serve Serena now. She has drunk from the elixir of life passed down from the elders and has promised to uphold good. I serve good," explained Eleganza.

"Be that as it may, I only serve myself," bawled Drakess merciless, then she cried out, "Puffin!"

Thereupon, Serena transformed into a far more ferocious and powerful dragon than anyone had ever set eyes on.

Unlike any other dragoness, Serena was luminous and powdered with silver stardust. As Drakess started to back away slowly, Serena the superior said, "You have my word, no one will harm you or Puffin. You will both be safe in this cavern. It is a time for forgiveness and for all living beings to live in harmony. Peace shall be brought to Tivarnia once again. I have foreseen it."

Drakess bowed before her not out of fear but out of respect. Puffin's cry could be heard from afar, which awoke Drakess's maternal instinct; her fury crumbled just like the rubble-filled caverns had done. She turned and fled, but only to embrace him like any other concerned mother would have done.

The day was saved not by the sword, but by the power of love and forgiveness.

# CHAPTER EIGHTEEN

## *Peace is Reborn*

Peace was restored once again in Tivarnia. To celebrate, festivities were held, and it was designated a national holiday, Peace Reborn Day, in remembrance of the Chosen One.

Freakadella was accepted back into the fairy community; furthermore, he was accepted for who he was. And so, it came to pass that no one was ever an outcast or felt alone in Tivarnia ever again. Everyone lived in harmony. Pleased with his new look, Freakadella mellowed; he was at peace with himself, but not because he looked more attractive on the outside but because he felt better on the inside. He learned that feeling good about oneself was all about self-acceptance and that it was inner beauty that counted the most. Having a good heart was far more beautiful than beauty itself, and it was eternal. Ultimately, being different wasn't a curse, for without variety life would be dull and Tivarnia surely would be tedious if everyone was the same.

Fairatella organised a coming out party for her uncle and everyone had lots of fairy fun, even Freakadella danced the night away in his high-heeled boots and sung

his heart out karaoke-style. Fairies do celebrate with a passion; it was a party full of glamour, illusion and magic, just what fairies do best!

The Tivarnian borders were no longer overgrown with intoxicating forget-me-nots, which induced deep sleep. Freakadella whole-heartedly released the spell, so all were free to come and go as they pleased. The fairies were no longer in danger of becoming a forgotten species. Fairatella organised her Fairy Mania Campaign and with fairy awareness at its peak, children learned of fairies as before and no more fairy lights went out. Tivarnia was the wish kingdom she had always dreamed of.

Freakadella undid all his evil witchcraft, all misfits became normal and their peculiarities disappeared in a puff of dragon smoke, except for Fairatella's, that is. She had to live out her other remaining eight lives before she could be an ordinary fairy. But did she mind? No, because she had come to realise that it was not a curse to be different, and she even encouraged others with her motto, "It's good to be different!" She even liked her tail, after all it did get her out of many tricky situations and having a hyper sense of smell came in handy too. Once freed of her inferiority complex, it dawned on her that she could fly just as well as any other fairy, despite her wings being smaller. The wings of light she sought in darkness before her task as the Chosen One were right behind her all the time; she was already wearing them. She had only to believe in herself to set her wings free. What really mattered was that she possessed a strong pair of wings.

Everyone was grateful for what Fairatella had achieved; she was Tivarnia's favourite heroine as she was so brave for one so tiny and had risked everything for Tivarnia. Fairatella was eminent as the Daystar, she shone bright like a true star. Even Tulipa and her so-called friends looked up to her. Over the course of time, they even became her real friends. They admired her for having an iron will that couldn't be broken; she never gave up no matter what.

No one ever suffered from harmful, verbal or physical abuse any more; Fairatella made sure of that by pointing out that those who feel inferior make the worst kind of bullies. In time, bullying became a forgotten word.

Daisy no longer had webbed feet; she spent most of her free time running around barefoot, merry, in the meadows. She was so proud of her sister Fairatella for being Tivarnia's most popular heroine, but more so for overcoming her fears, and she never stopped spontaneously reminding everyone of it.

Pan the tadpole grew into a handsome frog and was waiting to be kissed by a beautiful princess. He lived in the pond next door to The Tree That Was as before. Fairatella had picked him up on her way home from Dark Hollows; he was feeling so homesick that he didn't mind flying back.

Serena was as serene as ever, perhaps too serene. She tried to keep busy by upholding the peace, but really, she only ever had slight tiffs to deal with and almost wished for a little adventure. Since she had drunk from the elixir of life, sooner or later adventure would find her no doubt.

She remained young and beautiful and enjoyed her special bond with her goddaughter Fairatella.

Eleganza reminisced on her dragon days, sometimes with a fiery yearning, but she preferred having a clear conscious and flying light. Darting from one place to another, she was content being carefree, and lived her life without regrets. She continued being the fairies' steed and guided them beyond the mists of illusion, and on occasion she travelled between different dimensions as an agent of change.

Cantankerous Alexmeania got a canker from nibbling inappropriate substances. After trying hopelessly to quit her addiction, she at least managed to chew and nibble only on edible roots, especially ginger, which was good for her dyspepsia. She always kept a root or two handy in case a hunger pang struck and in doing so she actually lost weight. Tickled pink about her new size and being Tivarnia's most famous stepmother, she no longer envied Fairatella, as she was too busy being popular.

Silver coped better, too, seeing that Alexmeania was often absent and always too busy being popular to nag at him or pester him about trivial matters. He even endured her more, since she had become less cantankerous and kept her addiction under control. Funnily enough, in time, Alexmeania and Silver's relationship improved, and they weren't just keeping up appearances like before; they actually did get along much better and eventually they became close friends. He enjoyed his daughter's fame and popularity and of course being a famous father, but only because he was so proud of Fairatella and had only profuse praise for her endless accomplishments. It warmed him to believe that Bellarosea was also very proud of Fairatella, and he found peace knowing that he would reunite with his beloved wife someday. Thanks to Fairatella he was no longer wishing his time away; he was too preoccupied with Fae community affairs. Helping Fairatella reform Tivarnia had given him a reason to live; he got tremendous satisfaction knowing that his daughter, among all, was the Chosen One.

The secret wish that Fairatella had made that day in Yellow Meadows, to see Azaar again under better circumstances, came true. The special chemistry between them rekindled and love blossomed effortlessly. They opened their souls to one another and shared secrets and fears. Two kindred spirits bonded as fate had willed it. They had nothing to hide any more; she no longer felt embarrassed about her tail and she was even surprised to learn later that Azaar too had been a misfit, but he had hidden it well. Most of his body, especially his back, was covered with silky fur, so he was used to a furry touch and actually liked Fairatella stroking him gingerly with her tail or wrapping it around him, as it made him feel safe. Azaar vowed to love her for all his life and she hoped that would be for all her remaining lives, but she knew she couldn't fly away from her fate.

Everything was just as it should be in Tivarnia. Except that Fairatella missed Mr. Mumble Bee terribly, but she knew that life went on. It was Serena, a short time later, who helped her to realise that although she was capable of bending the space-time continuum to save Mr. Mumble

Bee, it would have serious consequences to do so, as it would change the sequence of events that took place afterwards, since he was one of the reasons she never gave up. However, since he was a figment of her imagination anyway, it was quite easy for her to think him up again.

"Make him reappear like magic," said Serena. "Imagine him rising from his ashes like a phoenix," she advised her. So Fairatella did just that, and the image of him emblazoned upon her mind, and *poof,* Mr. Mumble Bee wondrously emerged from his own ashes in the vigour of youth.

"Buzzz the beenix has risen!" mumbled Mr. Mumble Bee.

He annoyed her just like before at times, but she was always thankful that he did, as she never forgot what he had done for her, and that loyalty was the basis for any true friendship.

Here we come to the end of this fairy-tale. Fairatella the teller of tales would have wanted to say, "And they all lived fairly, happily, forever after," but for her it was just the beginning. She would have no end of tales to tell. Fairatella felt a profound appreciation for being alive and in fine fettle for a fairy, she wondered what other adventures awaited her in her next cat fairy lives, before becoming an ordinary fairy.

The End of the Beginning